The Trouble with Jack

Annie Seaton

Sunshine Coast Series: Book 1

ANNIE SEATON

This book is a work of fiction. Names, characters, places, and incidents are the product of the author's imagination or are used fictitiously. Any resemblance to actual events, locales, or persons, living or dead, is coincidental.

Originally published © 2014 by Annie Seaton as Brushing Off the Boss. All rights reserved, including the right to reproduce, distribute, or transmit in any form or by any means. For information regarding subsidiary rights, please contact the Publisher.

Second Edition: The Trouble with Jack, April 2020

ISBN: 978-0-6488742-4-9

Chapter One

The door of the Sea View Gallery at Noosa Heads shut with a satisfying *click* behind the last customer of the day, and Sienna Sacchi turned the closed sign around on the glass door.

"I thought she'd never leave." She yawned as she looked over to the electrician who was waiting to show her the new lighting he'd installed in the front corner of the gallery.

"But she was loaded with bags with the gallery insignia on them, if I'm not mistaken?" Jeremy waited for her to come over to the counter. "You were wasted in restoration, Sienna. You're a born saleswoman."

Sienna had been friends with Jeremy since school; the other business Sienna was involved with hired him for the electrical work. The restoration business—or house flipping as Georgie preferred to call it—was shared with

Georgie, her twin sister, and their best friend, Ana, up the mountain at Maleny. As well as working with the girls until recently, Sienna had also worked part-time in a small gallery up the mountain until she'd seen the ad for the gallery down here at Noosa.

"And a talented artist, too, don't forget." Sienna grinned at him as satisfaction coursed through her. A sale like the one she'd just made reassured her that her decision to be a silent partner in the reno business and move on to focus on her art and buy this gallery had been the right one. She would be her own boss once again; working for someone else stifled her creativity. "And yes, she loved my enamelled frogs, and bought one for each of her friends back in Sydney."

The sale had been one of the biggest Sienna had made since she'd taken over the management of the gallery a month ago. Her hiring had been done by email with the company and she hadn't even met the owner—the soon-to-be former owner; the gallery administration operated under a company name. Once she owned the place, she would have final say in how it was run. She couldn't wait to tell the girls; she'd told Georgie she had news but wouldn't give any clues away.

"That's the sort of customer you want." Jeremy looked at her with a grin. "Holy Dooley, I saw the price tag on your frogs when I was running the electrical wires under the shelves."

Sienna nodded with a smile. "So, are you done?"

"I am. Are you ready to be bedazzled?"

"I am." Sienna had filled the corner at the front of the gallery with her own work. She waited as Jeremy stepped behind the elegant glass table she used as a counter, reached down, and flicked a switch.

Sienna gasped and put her hands to her lips as she surveyed the once-dark corner. The various little creatures came to life on the display shelves along the side wall. Colourful frogs peeked from behind small pieces of wood softly lit by downlights hidden beneath the higher shelves, and copper grasshoppers gleamed in the corners. She had been working day and night to finish her sculpted metal creatures for her upcoming exhibition, but she still had a lot of work ahead.

"Happy with the job then, sweets?"

"Happy? I'm delighted. It's like fairyland." The small creatures she had enamelled in bright primary colours were highlighted by the carefully placed lighting. She stepped closer and twirled around, looking at the lights as they twinkled, and was hard pressed not to yell out in delight. "You've worked magic, Jeremy. Thank you so much."

"My pleasure." He picked up his toolbox and crossed to the door. "I won't bill the company until I finish the whole room for your exhibition. Let me know when you want me to come back."

After he left, Sienna wandered around, barely able to keep the smile off her face. The gallery looked very different from when she'd taken over as manager, with an option to purchase, only four weeks ago. The last email from a secretary at the company advised that any changes she made before the contract was signed must be approved and then would be billed out to the company. It had taken three weeks to get the approval to go ahead with the lighting, and she'd worried it wouldn't be complete before her exhibition. As soon as she'd received an email giving her the go-ahead, she'd called Jeremy to come in to do the work, and he'd turned up within an hour.

There'd been no reply from her solicitor about the contract of sale when she'd checked her email at lunchtime; she glanced down at her watch. Hopefully it would settle next week, and then the gallery would be all hers with the freedom to do as she wanted before her first exhibition. Having to get permission to make any change, no matter how small, was a pain in the proverbial.

There was no time to check her email before she left for the restaurant. As usual Sienna was running late, and she knew the girls would tease her about being late for her own birthday dinner.

She grabbed her iPad and her bag from beneath the counter, and with one last satisfied smile at the beautifully lit display, she flicked the lights off and headed for the back door.

Chapter Two

The waiter leaned over the table and the cork popped out of the champagne bottle flying over the heads of the patrons in the noisy, crowded restaurant. Sienna laughed and leaned forward, holding her glass to catch the cascading bubbles.

"Happy birthday!" Ana took Sienna's glass as wine frothed over the top onto the checked tablecloth.

Georgie mopped at the damp cloth with her napkin and smiled at Sienna. "Happy birthday, sis."

"You too, Georgie." Sienna grinned back, wondering for the millionth time how they could be so different. Even though they were fraternal twins, in twenty-nine years she had never been able to find one glimmer of similarity between them.

Looks, personality, interests, or attitudes. About the only thing they shared was their birthday.

"So, Machu Picchu is still the plan for next year's big thirty?" Ana, their best friend since primary school up the mountain at Maleny, sipped her wine. Sienna and Georgie had always promised themselves a special trip for their thirtieth birthday, even if they were married with kids. But that hadn't happened for either of them—intentionally for Sienna, and not so intentionally for Georgie.

Sienna shook her head and looked across at her twin. Georgie was leaning into her latest boyfriend, Cal . . . or something? Kel?

She couldn't keep up with the men in Georgie's life. Her sister always tried so hard to find Mr. Right. Each time a guy sensed Georgie was after the wedding dress dream, he took off and she was left nursing another broken heart.

She should know by now relationships rarely work out, and she needs to toughen up, Sienna thought, but kept her thoughts to herself

Georgie caught her eye and smiled. "No, Sienna will be too busy. Are you going to tell us your news, sis?

Sienna rose to her feet and tapped her glass with a spoon, but the hum of noise from the other patrons in Fish Divine overlooking the beach at Noosa covered the sound. She sat back down with a grin and waited until she had the attention of the small group at the table. Leaning back on her chair, she lifted her glass and sipped before she announced in a dramatic voice, "I *almost* have news."

"Come on, don't keep us in suspense." Ana leaned forward and placed her elbows on the table. Sienna hadn't caught up with the girls since she'd moved to the gallery at Noosa.

"You know how much I loved working at the gallery at Maleny?" she said.

Ana nodded, and Georgie smiled.

"Well, I quit." Sienna knew she had a flair for drama; Georgie had always said she should go into the movies.

"What?" Ana frowned. "I thought you were about to have an exhibition of your sculptures?"

"I was, but my sculptures and I have moved to the Sea View Gallery up the road here." Sienna picked up her glass and sipped. "And the big news is—I'm about to buy it. I will have my very own gallery. I'm just waiting to hear when I sign the contract."

She waited for their congratulations, but Ana looked at her with a strange expression on her face, almost disbelief. "Did you say the Sea View Gallery?"

"Yes. It's in a much better location than Maleny. I mean I know there were a lot of tourists up the mountain, but this so much busier. I'm really excited. You know I've always dreamed about having my own gallery. All that hard work in our restoration business has paid off. I'll have my own place where I can show my work. And I can run it how *I* want."

Still no flurry of congratulations.

"And you'll all get a special invitation to my first show at the end of the month."

It wasn't like Ana to be so quiet. Sienna frowned at her across the table.

"What's wrong, Ana? Aren't you just a little bit excited for me?"

Ana reached out across the table and grabbed Sienna's hand. "Sweetie, there's something you need to—"

"Is this a private party, or can anyone join?"

Sienna froze and her heartbeat kicked up a notch before she turned slowly. She'd know that voice anywhere. A delicious shiver ran down her back as she looked up at Jack Montgomery who was standing behind her chair. Ever since she'd first met him last year when he was visiting the area with Blake, Ana's partner, her interest had increased each time they'd run into each other.

Blake had ended up buying the Maleny hardware store and Jack had been a visitor for a while, but he'd never stayed long enough to take Sienna out for dinner like he'd mentioned a few times. Last she'd heard from Ana, he was in Melbourne looking after the family company. His bad-boy reputation had piqued her interest, although Ana assured her, he had settled down since his dad had been ill.

"I told Blake I was coming to town, and he invited me to join you." Jack looked around with a frown. "Where is he?"

"Blake had to cancel." Ana gestured to the chair beside her and Sienna bit her lip, as a ripple of disappointment ran through her; she'd been about to invite Jack to sit beside her.

"There was a crisis at the store, and he asked me to look out for you, Jack," Ana said.

"So, he hasn't changed his workaholic ways yet? Even though he's moved from big business to a small store of his own? I think I've won a bet there." Jack pulled out the chair and sat beside Ana, but his intent gaze was fixed on Sienna, and her heart felt like it was doing backflips in her chest.

"I'll have to line him up for a game of golf or two." Jack didn't take his eyes from her.

She swallowed and flicked her scarf back over her shoulder, trying to regain her composure. He was the only man who ever made her nervous. "How are you, Jack? You haven't been up this way for a while," she said trying to look calmer than she felt.

"I'm well, thanks." Jack kept his green-eyed gaze on her, and his sexy grin sent another shiver down her back. "Especially now that I'm moving here for good. We must catch up."

"We must." She smiled and a frisson of anticipation shot through her in a lazy swirl.

Woo hoo. Life's looking good. Jack's back on the scene; I'll have my own gallery and an exhibition coming up.

Ana put her hand over her mouth and cleared her throat loudly before Jack answered. Her brow was wrinkled in a frown and she stared at Sienna.

What's going on?

The noise of the conversations in the restaurant washed over her as Sienna moved her gaze from Ana back to Jack. He would make a good subject for a portrait; her fingers tingled with the urge to capture his face on canvas. It would be a happy portrait of a man at ease in his own skin. Jack always had that sexy grin on his face. He had high, sharply defined cheekbones, and sensuous lips that were tilted up in a smile as he looked back at her. His sun-streaked hair flopped onto his forehead, and the come-hither eyes fixed on her were enough to give her palpitations. Having him back on the coast might prove to be very interesting…and a lot of fun.

"Sienna?" Ana's soft voice pulled her from her dreamy musing. "Come for a walk with me?" Ana looked across at Jack apologetically. "Please excuse us for a minute."

"Excuse me." Sienna pushed her chair back and caught Jack's eye. This time the tingle that ran through her was warm and settled nicely in her tummy. "I'm pleased you were able to come tonight." She ran her hand lightly down his arm as she passed by his chair, and his warm skin beneath her fingers kept those tingles going.

This is going to be fun. I'm overdue for some, that's for sure.

As she followed Ana to the ladies' room, thoughts of Jack and the launch she'd planned once the gallery was hers filled her head. She'd invite him . . .

Ana kept walking past the ladies' room before she pushed open the door of the restaurant that led out onto Hastings Street..

"What's up? Where are we going?" Sienna followed her until they reached the gap between the buildings where there was an excellent view of the beach

Ana leaned against the white timber wall, her back to the view. She grabbed Sienna's hands; unease caught in her throat as Ana held them. "I need to tell you something before you put your foot in it with Jack."

"What do you mean? What's wrong?"

"I so wish you'd told me you were at the Sea View Gallery and wanting to buy it. I know you keep things close to your chest, you always have, but you are going to be so disappointed."

"What on earth are you talking about? Stop talking in riddles." She stared at Ana.

"The gallery's not for sale anymore."

"How could you possibly know that?"

"Jack called Blake last night. Now that his father has recovered, Jack can hand the family business back over. He never wanted to be there in the first place." Ana held Sienna's gaze and squeezed her hands. "He's moved here to run another business *his* company bought a couple of years ago. An art gallery. The *Sea View* Gallery."

***

Jack leaned back in his chair and watched as Sienna and Ana headed for the door. Sienna was even prettier than he'd remembered. She was wearing a tight-fitting black top tucked into a coloured floaty skirt. A matching scarf hung around her long slender neck His blood zinged in appreciation. Sienna had fascinated him from the moment they met, and he knew the attraction was mutual. He'd always intended on asking her out but getting called back to Melbourne when his father got sick had put that on hold. Tonight, he'd pick up where he'd left off last year.

"So, you're really here to stay this time?" Georgie smiled at him, and Jack shot a glance at the guy who was sitting on the other side of her. He held his hand out across the table.

"Jack Montgomery."

"Sorry, how rude of me. I didn't introduce you." Georgie said. "This is my friend Cole. He just started work at the hardware store in Maleny."

Cole shot him a sullen look as Jack shook his hand.

What's his problem?

Jack turned away from the guy with the death stare to speak to Georgie. "It's good to be back on the Sunny Coast. When I told Blake I was arriving today, he said you'd all be down here tonight."

"We came to celebrate our birthday. Sienna and I, that is." Georgie shot him a grin. "Where are you staying? In Noosa?"

"Yes, in my gallery. I swung by there and threw my bag in on the way. There's a sofa at the back of the studio, and that'll do for a while. At least I hope there is. I only had a quick look at the place when I bought it. It's been managed by Dad's company for a couple of years." Jack stifled a yawn. "Sorry. I left Melbourne the day before yesterday, and I rode my bike up from Sydney today. Left at the crack of dawn."

"That's a long haul. What kind of bike have you got?" Cole took his arm from around Georgie's shoulder and leaned forward.

"A BMW K1600GT. Best one I've ever had." He glanced at Georgie as she moved her chair a little closer to his. "And I've had a few."

The guy was giving him bad vibes.

"What gallery are you talking about?" she asked.

"The Sea View Gallery in Hastings Drive. I bought it around the same time that Ana hooked up with Blake." Jack settled back in his chair and glanced around, wondering where Sienna and Ana had disappeared to. "I had it on the market, but now I've decided to move here and use it as my base. Try my hand with my own gallery and doing something I love."

Georgie's eyes widened and she grabbed Jack's arm. "Did you say the Sea View Gallery? Here? In Noosa?"

"I did. Why? Is something wrong?"

"Oh, shit," she said.

Ana held the door open and Sienna strode in. Her black hair was cut short, framing her face in a pixie cut. Her dark brown eyes looked huge, outlined with that black pencil stuff she always wore. She flopped into her chair and sat back with her arms folded and stared across the table at Jack.

Her gaze was not friendly, and tension fair radiated off her. Jack looked from Sienna and back to Georgie, unsure of the vibes he was picking up.

"Happy birthday. If I'd known this was a birthday party, I wouldn't have intruded." He looked around for the waiter. "The least I can do is buy a bottle of champagne."

"I'll get it. The waitress is busy." Sienna stood and pushed her chair back hard. It hit the low windowsill behind her with a loud *crack*.

Jack slid his chair back and followed her to the bar at the other end of the restaurant. She was edgy, and it seemed as though she was trying to get away from him. It was strange because five minutes ago she'd been smiling back at him. As they waited behind another couple, he took hold of her arm. "Would you like to tell me what I've done to upset you?"

"No, I wouldn't." Sienna stared up at him without a smile. He could have sworn her voice broke slightly, and she turned away from him and stared through the window. The sun had slipped below the horizon, and fingers of mist were settling over the street as the sky darkened.

Jack shrugged and gave his order to the barman. The tension rolling off Sienna was enough to make him fidget as he waited for the bartender to open the champagne. Finally, the bottle was on the bar in front of him. "Coming?" He grabbed the bottle and waited for her to follow.

"I'll be there in a minute." It was quite clear she didn't want to be in his company.

"Fair enough." Jack shrugged.

On his way back to the table, Cole pushed past him as he headed for the bar. Jack placed the bottle in the wine bucket and glanced back just in time to see the guy lean into Sienna. He put his hand on her waist, and she shoved it away. Jack's fists curled as words were exchanged, and Cole glared at her for a few seconds before he pushed past her and headed for the door. Georgie and Ana, deep in conversation, missed the whole interaction.

Sienna walked back to the table, a flush on her cheeks.

"Everything okay?" Jack kept his voice low as she returned to her chair, a surge of protection rising in him.

"Bloody perfect." She waited until Georgie looked across at her. "Your friend had to leave suddenly. I'll explain later."

Jack was bemused when conversation turned to the hardware store.

"Magda came in the other day." Georgie held out her glass for a top-up and smiled at him. "She and Joe are leaving for a Pacific cruise next week."

Ana turned to Jack to include him in the conversation. "Did you ever meet them? They are the sweetest old couple. They've lived in Maleny forever. Blake bought the hardware store from them when he left your father's company."

Jack shook his head.

"How many cruises have Joe and Magda been on now?" Ana asked Georgie.

The conversation buzzed around Jack and it was as though he'd imagined the prickly atmosphere when Ana and Sienna came inside, and the interaction he'd just witnessed at the bar. He sat back, interested to catch up with all their news. He hadn't been north for over a year. He'd stayed in Melbourne to support his mother after his father's heart attack. To his surprise, she stepped in to help him with the company while Dad went through a series of heart operations and a massive lifestyle change. In the end, to his great relief, Jack had only had to play a minor role in the business, and he'd spent a lot of time with his father. Dad had disapproved of his casual attitude and frowned at the playboy lifestyle he thought Jack led. They'd had a few rocky years, and finally made their peace after Dad finally understood that Jack's creative nature didn't lend itself to being in big business, and Jack had spent more time on his art and less time hitting the clubs.

When Dad had offered for his company to manage the gallery for him, Jack had viewed it merely as Dad investing in something Jack loved. Now he had a chance, once and for all, to prove to his father that art was not a hobby, but his lifetime career. Getting the commission for his sculptures in a new building in Sydney had built Jack's confidence, but until he'd finished them and met the deadline, he was not going to tell anyone why he'd moved here. He would prove to everyone that he was a true artist and that the commission had not been a fluke, no matter what Dad said. There had been an offer to buy the gallery last month, but he'd told the management company to tell the buyer it was no longer for sale. He had something to prove to himself.

This was Jack's big chance to make something of himself in the art world.

Something that hasn't been given to me.

There was no way he would ever get sucked into letting money rule *his* life. Chasing the dollar almost killed his father, and he had no life outside of his work.

Not for me. No way.

"Sir?" Jack looked up at the waitress who was standing beside him, with her order pad ready.

"I'll just have the seafood chowder, thanks." Jack stifled a yawn. "Sorry. I need to have an early night and grab some sleep."

He caught Sienna looking at him as he reached for his water glass. If he drank any wine, he'd probably fall asleep at the table.

"You do look tired." Her voice had lost the icy edge and the angry colour on her cheekbones had faded. Maybe it was that other guy who had been bugging her.

"Yeah, I love riding my bike, but the last two days were pretty hectic. I wanted to get up to the coast to—"

"Well, it's good to see you here." Sienna cut him off before he could finish. "I'm sure we'll be catching up some more."

"Hope so. Are you still working in Maleny?" He'd assumed that Sienna still worked in the hardware store where they'd first met.

"No," she said slowly. "I've moved jobs down this way." She held his gaze, her beautiful dark eyes fixed on his.

He lowered his voice. "I'll give you a call later in the week when I get settled. Same number?"

Sienna looked at him over the top of her glass, but her expression was guarded as she nodded slowly. "Same number."

Georgie cleared her throat loudly, and he reluctantly broke eye contact with Sienna and settled back in his chair.

"Don't drown like our great-grandmother. That was one of Uncle Renzo's favourite stories," Georgie said. Jack looked across the table at her as her laugh rang out, before he switched his gaze back to Sienna. Damn it, he couldn't take his eyes off her. Sienna had a wry grin on her face.

"And you, as gullible as usual, always fell for Uncle Renzo's story," she said, nudging Georgie with her elbow.

Jack must have looked confused, and Sienna leaned closer to him as she explained. Her perfume was sharp and floral, and he took a deep breath, enjoying the fresh fragrance after a day on the road smelling dust and bitumen.

"When we were in high school, Uncle Renzo brought us down here to the beach at Noosa for a birthday dinner, and he told Georgie a story about his grandmother falling asleep at the table when he was a little boy and drowning in her seafood chowder."

Jack grinned as Sienna continued the story. "He had her sucked in, hook, line and sinker, for the whole night until she started to cry, and then he took pity on her."

Sienna smiled as she looked at Jack. Her long, delicate neck arched gracefully as her head turned slowly from side to side, and he got another whiff of her perfume. Her eyes were hooded, and Jack sensed she was waiting for something.

Or someone, maybe?

He couldn't smother the next yawn that overtook him when he finished his meal. Jack pushed his plate away and put his hand over his mouth. "Sorry."

"Boring you, are we?" Sienna smiled, and he held her gaze for a long time before she looked down again. Her long dark lashes hid her expression.

"Not in the least, but I'll have to get some sleep, or I'll drown in the chowder too." He joked to lighten the tension between them; you could almost hear the attraction crackling between them. He was looking forward to spending time with her, as soon as he got himself organised.

"I hear you've been in business back in Melbourne." Sienna tipped her head on the side and narrowed her eyes.

"Yeah, I have been. But it wasn't really my scene. I'm sure I'm going to like the Sunshine Coast much better than the hectic pace of Melbourne."

"It can get hectic here too," she said, and there was something strange in her tone, as though she was trying to talk him out of the move. Jack racked his brains trying to think how much Blake knew of his reasons for coming down here. He knew he owned the gallery but nothing else. No one else knew about his commission.

"So, you didn't like being the boss? You're going to do that sort of thing down here?" Sienna sounded interested.

"No, I'm not." Jack shrugged. "I intend on finding a good manager for my business and I'll look for a place to live near the beach. I'm sure I'll get plenty of time to go surfing."

"I hear it's hard to get good staff down this way." Sienna glanced at him and he had the feeling she disapproved of his plans.

Jack narrowed his eyes; he didn't need anyone else judging him. "Is it? I'm sure I'll find an agency to help me." It was as though they were playing a game, but he didn't have a clue what it was.

"So, bring me up to date. Are you all still in the restoration business?"

Ana and Georgie shook their heads, but it was Sienna who answered him.

"I suppose you could call my *work* that. I still work with 'doohickeys' of a sort." She sat up straight in her chair and her voice was still a bit snarky. He wasn't imagining it; she was playing games with him and he didn't like it.

Maybe he wouldn't call her after all. He didn't need any unnecessary complications taking up his time.

Jack put a civil smile on his face. "That's right. I'd forgotten the slogan for that hardware store that Blake bought. What was it again?"

"*Whatchamacallits, thingamajigs, and doohickeys for every need*," Georgie piped up. She and Ana had been watching the interaction between Jack and Sienna with interest.

Why did he get the feeling that everyone else knew what was going on? It was hard to concentrate because he was so tired from the long ride today.

Jack pushed his chair back and stood slowly, but Sienna's eyes stayed on him. "Time I hit the road. You'll have to excuse me. I've had a long day." Jack turned to Ana and Georgie and smiled. "I'm sure we'll catch up in Maleny. I'll be up to see Blake in the next couple of weeks. As soon as I get settled, I'll give him a call."

Sienna lifted her wineglass to her lips and sipped slowly, regarding him over the rim.

"I'll give you a call too, Sienna." Jack's eyes fixed on her rosy lips until her next words dripped from them.

"I'll look forward to it." But her terse tone belied the words. Jack turned to ask for the bill, but Sienna's next words stopped him.

"Tell me, Jack, whatever possessed you to buy an art gallery when you've had nothing to do with the art world?"

So, she wanted to be smart. Well, he could play the same game. He turned slowly to face her.

"A gallery just sells a different type of product. Business is business whatever is sold. Paintings, pottery, furniture, wheelbarrows, stocks and shares…even doohickeys"—he flicked a glance at her— "or whatever it was you were in charge of in that hardware store. As long as you have a buyer and decent staff, there's money to be made. No knowledge of art required."

They were his father's words, and although Jack didn't believe them for a moment, he made them his. Sienna had really pushed his buttons with her "nothing to do with the art world" comment.

Her eyes flashed at him as her cheeks coloured a deep red. "Well, Jack, I'm sure your *staff* will look after your gallery and make lots of money for you while you're off surfing."

"That's all I can hope for." He caught the waitress's eye and asked for the check before turning back to the table. "I'll get the bill—that's my gift to you both. I hope you had a happy birthday, ladies."

The scowl on Sienna's face said otherwise.

Chapter Three

"What did you say to Cole to upset him?" Georgie stood outside the door of the restaurant with Sienna, while Ana went to the ladies. "Why did he leave?"

"Why would you think it was me who upset *him*?" Sienna didn't let the hurt show in her tone. She kept her voice firm as she faced her sister. "He made a move on me."

"I can really pick 'em, can't I?" Georgie frowned. "I can't believe he hit on you on our second date. I'm destined to be a spinster. I might as well move in with the surrogate great-aunts now.

Sienna shook her head with a small smile before she looped her arm around her twin's shoulder. "I don't think you're quite ready for crocheting coat hangers with Thelma and Mitzi just yet. You just have to toughen up."

"You're not as tough as you make out." Georgie gave her a sideways glance. "I saw the way you were trying to act mean with Jack, but you can't fool me. You're as soft as marshmallow inside. I'll just focus on my job for a while, pay off my apartment, and then I'm going to travel. We might make Machu Picchu together yet." She punched Sienna lightly on the top of her arm. "And then when I get back, we can both move in with the aunts and you can paint the toilet roll holders."

"Very funny," Sienna said drily. "I've got grander plans than that for my art." She stifled a giggle. "Although I suppose the toilet roll holders are products too. A bit quirky. Maybe we could ask Jack to sell them in the gallery. After all, what did he say? Wheelbarrows, stocks and shares…even doohickeys."

"I'm pleased to see your sense of humour is back," Georgie said. She turned to Ana. "I guess I need a lift home, seeing as my sweet sister here sent my driver home without me. Can you drop me off?"

Ana nodded and the three girls headed off along Hastings Street together in a comfortable silence. The air was crisp as the chill of the autumn air settled, and Sienna took a deep breath when the salt-tanged breeze drifted across from the beach. She opened her bag and pulled out her keys. "I'll see you all next weekend?"

"Whoa, not so fast." Ana grabbed her arm. "We need to talk."

"What about?" Sienna wanted to get home and think about the bombshell that Ana had dropped about Jack being the owner of the gallery . . . *her* gallery.

"Are you okay? About the gallery?" Ana frowned.

"Yes, I'm okay."

The gut-wrenching disappointment that had hit her when Ana told her about Jack owning the gallery, and changing his mind about selling, settled in Sienna's stomach like a stone. She worried about the schedule for her exhibition. She needed to keep using the studio to finish her pieces in time. She'd done so much preparation; the exhibition couldn't be put back. To make matters worse was the jolt that hit her nerve endings, *everywhere,* every time Jack looked at her or opened his mouth to speak and let that sexy voice pour over her. If he was going to be her boss, seeing him was out of the question. Besides, all her energy right now had to go into finishing her pieces and setting up the exhibition. She had no time for a social life—and didn't want to ruin her reputation in the art community by going out with the boss. Funny that, until she'd found out Jack owned the gallery, she had looked forward to catching up and having some fun.

Sea View Gallery was perfect for her, and the building had everything that she wanted. This afternoon seemed like a dream now; she'd had such plans for the place. It had the best position—on one of the busiest tourist streets in Queensland. As well as that it was a great building: it had the best layout, with a kiln room underneath, it was across from the beach; and she'd already started to change the interior. And not only that, she was using the studio at the back for her work. She'd even slept on the sofa in the studio a few nights when she was too tired to drive to the lake. She'd been planning on spending all day there tomorrow to do some more enamelling of her frogs.

But she didn't want to worry Georgie and Ana. "It's okay. Another space will come up for sale eventually."

"I was worried you'd be really disappointed." Ana reached over and kissed her cheek. "We'll catch up soon. I'd better hurry up and pick Faith up. She'll have worn out the old dears by now. I know Thelma and Mitzi love her, but they spoil that daughter of ours dreadfully. They wanted to know if we were ever getting married so she could be the flower girl. Would you believe they started pulling out dresses from *their* grandmother's time?"

"So . . . is there going to be a wedding?" Sienna smiled at her friend.

"Of course there is . . . one day. And you two will be the first to find out when." Ana grinned, and then headed for her car.

"I'll be there in a minute." Georgie waited with Sienna and turned to her with a frown. "You're devastated about the gallery, aren't you? I know you very well, sister dear."

Sienna linked her arm through her twin's. "That's a bit over the top. Not devastated, but I am disappointed. I had such big plans for it."

"I could see the sparks snapping between you and Jack. I told the soup story to kill the sexual tension that was hanging over the table. Now you have to work for him."

"If he won't sell to me, I'll find something else. I haven't given up on the idea." Sienna sighed. "I don't want to have to ask approval for everything I do. I just hope I can still have my exhibition at the end of the month. Maybe I can find a vacant shop in Caloundra or Mooloolaba."

Georgie stared at her. "Noosa is the artsy capital of the Queensland coast. Don't give up so easily. Maybe he won't come in and change things."

"I'll think about it." Sienna leaned over and hugged Georgie. "Between sleazy Cole and sexy Jack, we certainly had an eventful birthday."

"Just don't make any hasty decisions. I know how much time you've invested in this exhibition." A phone beeped loudly. Georgie unzipped her bag and scrabbled around in it. "Blasted phone. It always gets lost in this bag. Got you, you little sucker." She blew Sienna a kiss before she hitched her bag back onto her shoulder and glanced down at the screen.

"A text from Cole." She shoved the phone back in her bag and turned toward Ana's car.

"Georgie?" Sienna put her hand on her sister's arm as she moved away.

"Uh-oh." Georgie rolled her eyes. "You've got the big-sister lecture face on."

"I know we joke about it, but promise me you'll be a little bit more . . . er . . . careful when you accept a date next time?"

"I know, he was a sleaze but—"

"Stop trying so hard. There's no such thing as happy ever after." Sienna crossed her arms, waiting for Georgie's reaction.

"You are so cynical. I do worry about you." Georgie frowned and rubbed her forehead with her hand. "Romance is alive and well. Look at Ana and Blake. Look at all the lovely old couples in Maleny who've been married for a hundred years."

"A hundred?" Sienna looked away at the fog rolling in from the sea. "Ana and Blake, well, they're one in a million. You've got to stop going out with losers just to try to find something that doesn't exist."

"Just because our mother made bad choices doesn't mean we can't find love. *You* have to learn to trust."

Sienna pushed away the sympathy that rose in her chest when she saw tears well up in Georgie's eyes. Her twin was going to end up hurt . . . again.

"I don't *need* to be loved by a man. It's not what I want. I love what I do and I'm really happy with my life the way it is." She shook her head as the disappointment of the night's events resurfaced. "If it hadn't been for Jack changing his mind about selling the gallery, I would have been well on my way to being settled. But I'll find something else."

"Well, we're going to have to agree to disagree again." Georgie's face was closed, and she turned away. "I'd better hurry, Ana's waiting. So no hasty decisions about the gallery, especially if Jack lets you keep the date for the show. Okay?"

Sienna waved as she walked over to her car parked two rows away.

"I promise," she said.

She would have to catch up with Jack first thing on Monday and find out what was happening. It was strange that no one from the company had even contacted her to say he was coming.

Chapter Four

Jack rolled the BMW up to the kerb a couple of doors up the street from the gallery. He knew there was a garage behind the building, but he only had a key to the front door. The rest of the keys had always been with the manager.

He let himself in and felt around for a light switch. There was a full moon to help light his way; the streetlight was outside the dress shop next door. He flicked the switch and shelves were bathed in a soft light; a brighter spotlight highlighted a colourful display in the window. The space was well laid out and looked very different from when he'd first bought the place. He'd run the numbers, ducked into the gallery for a quick look, and realised the property would appreciate in value. Its location was one of the best in the street. So he'd bought it and left it in the hands of Dad's company, which looked after a few of his interests.

Whoever was managing it now was doing it well. He hoped the current manager would stay on. He didn't want a full-time role running the place. His deadline was coming up fast, and he was itching to get back to his sculpting when his stuff arrived next week.

A stack of work to do before I can get those pieces finished.

Jack grabbed the bag he'd thrown in the door earlier and wandered around, picking up the occasional piece on display. Vases, bowls, all with a motif of small animals and insects, as well as an eclectic array of pieces, filled the shelves. And the colour followed a pattern that appealed to his sense of order. Everything in the window facing the street was in bright primary colours and bathed in the strongest light. As he let his gaze wander down along the shelves to the back of the gallery, he appreciated the skill that had gone into the placement of the pieces by colour. Mid-range yellows and greens filled the middle shelves and were lit with a fading light. At the back of the gallery, set in an alcove, white bowls were set off by a soft light shining down from beneath the low ceiling. Candles and bowls of flower petals placed discreetly between the artwork gave off a soft floral fragrance.

Very nicely done. It was well balanced. If the manger was that good, he might even think about a pay rise.

Jack yawned and a muscle tightened between his shoulders. He tipped his head to the side to stretch his neck. If he didn't get some sleep, he'd be useless tomorrow. At least it was Sunday and the gallery would be closed, according to the discreet sign on the glass counter near the door. He switched off the lights and pushed open the door at the back, which opened into a small kitchen. Two more doors were at the back of the kitchen. Jack pushed open the first, nodding with satisfaction as he took in a small bathroom.

Putting his bag on the floor, he pulled his T-shirt over his head and ran water over his face in the small sink. He wiped his face and hands on his T-shirt before he pushed open the last door. It opened into a studio filled with shadows, but the moonlight streaming in through the large bay window facing north hinted at the light that would fill the room in the daytime.

Too tired to turn on the light and lift all the drop sheets covering the shelves to see what was beneath them, Jack headed over to the sofa tucked into the back corner of the room. Thank goodness he didn't have to crash on the floor, although he was so tired, he could have slept anywhere. He threw his T-shirt onto the floor before he stepped out of his jeans and kicked them aside.

A blanket was draped over the back of the sofa, and he sank gratefully into the soft cushions and closed his eyes. As sleep overtook him, he forgot about the gallery and all his plans; his artist's eye took him back to Sienna, with her large dark eyes made bigger by black kohl, accentuated by the short feathery hair just touching the fair skin on her forehead. Her high cheekbones had worn a soft flush throughout dinner, and a sexy smile had tilted her rosebud lips before her mood had changed. Jack drifted off and sleep overtook him with Sienna's face planted firmly in his thoughts. He could even smell her perfume.

###

Jack couldn't be sure if it was the light streaming through the bay window or the need for coffee that roused him from a deep sleep hours later. He swung his legs over the sofa and leaned forward, rubbing his hands over his stubbled chin. He'd go in search of that much-needed coffee as soon as he shaved and showered. He looked down at his watch. It was only seven o'clock; he was sure he'd find an open restaurant close by in a tourist town like Noosa.

Coffee . . . and eggs. Or pancakes. Or both. With bacon.

Jack lifted his head at the sound of dishes, and he realised he really could smell coffee.

It's not just wishful thinking.

He quickly retrieved his jeans from the floor and stepped into them before he walked across to the door. He lifted his hand to turn the knob, but the door opened in front of him before he reached it.

"Shit a brick," he exclaimed.

A hot cup of coffee hit his bare chest at the same time Sienna's squeal reached his ears. He jumped back when the mug tipped over and hot coffee spilled all over the wooden floor. The cup bounced without breaking.

"What on earth are you doing here? And bringing me coffee? Are you a mind reader?" He rubbed his eyes and looked at Sienna, trying to figure out what the hell she was doing here. "Or am I still dreaming?"

"What?" Sienna gawked back at him.

"How did you know I was here?" Jack racked his brain trying to remember the conversation last night. "And how did you get in? Did I forget to lock the door?" He rubbed his hands over his eyes again trying to wake up. He stepped across the room and picked up his T-shirt and pulled it over his head. Sienna just stood there looking at him, not saying a word.

He walked back over and took her arm. "Sorry. You woke me up. I didn't even check to see if you were okay. That coffee didn't burn you, did it?"

"No, I'm fine." She pulled back from him and folded her arms. Jack looked down, following the direction of her gaze. He grinned and zipped up his jeans over his black boxers before he reached out and gently held her shoulders.

"It was very sweet of you to bring me coffee. Did Georgie tell you I was here?"

Beneath his hands, Sienna put her shoulders back. Her muscles tensed when she took a deep breath. "Let's just get one thing clear, mister. One thing I am not . . . is sweet."

"But you brought me coffee?" He grinned at her.

"In your dreams." But a smile hovered at the corner of her mouth.

Jack dropped his hands and shook his head in confusion. "So what are you doing here?"

He stepped back to give her some space, taking care to avoid the puddle of coffee on the floor around them.

Sienna looked him up and down, her expression serious. "I manage the gallery. Or at least I did. It depends on what the *owner*"— emphasis on the word, and she lifted her chin— "wants to do now that he has a sudden interest in the place."

"You're my manager? You're going to be working for *me*? Are you serious? Why didn't you tell me that last night?" Jack narrowed his eyes and grabbed her hand. "What are you doing here on a Sunday? The gallery is closed, isn't it"

"Which of your twenty questions will I answer first?" Sienna tipped her head to the side and she regarded him steadily. "Don't make assumptions about me. I'm more than a shop assistant. I manage everything about the gallery, and I work here in the studio. And I *was* in the middle of purchasing the place." Sienna pulled her hand away and flicked a graceful hand around the studio. "This is—or was—my studio. I've always been an artist even when I worked for the hardware store, and when I worked with the girls Oh, and yes . . . we are closed Sundays."

He stared back; she really had the dirts this morning. "I'm sorry. I seem to have made more than one wrong assumption." Jack ran his hand through his hair. "Didn't you know I own the place? Ah"—he tapped his hand on his forehead— "that's what was wrong with you at dinner last night."

"I only found out last night. I'd emailed my lawyer to take up the option to buy and I was waiting to hear back. No one told me you owned it and were coming back. Ana told me when you arrived."

"That explains why you were so snaky last night." Jack pulled out his best killer smile, but it didn't seem to work. Sienna stood next to the door, her arms folded, and her beautiful face darkened by that same scowl.

"There's obviously been a mix-up. I'm sorry." Jack shrugged. There wasn't a lot more he could do.

"Obviously," she said.

"Look, can we start again?" Jack held out his hand, but Sienna ignored it. He had no idea what she was thinking. The serious face in front of him was nothing like the sweet one that had filled his mind as he'd gone to sleep last night. Then her words filtered through to his sluggish brain. "What sort of artist?"

"Later." Sienna turned on her heel and waved her hand as she headed to the door. "Have a shower or whatever. I'll clean up that coffee, and then you can tell me your plans for the place."

The door closed behind her with a loud *click* and Jack shook his head, totally bemused.

An artist? And she said she'd been going to buy the gallery. Something was amiss. Jack walked back to the sofa and sat down. He ran a hand across his eyes, trying to dispel the feeling that things had gone awry, before he grabbed a towel from his bag and headed for a shower. Maybe it'd clear his head a bit. Tomorrow, he'd make some calls and find out where the stuff up had happened.

There was no sign of Sienna when he went through the kitchen on the way to the small bathroom. Jack stood beneath the water, turning the temperature to cool, trying to wake up. If she was using the studio here, there were going to have to be changes. He needed this studio for his work, and his deadline meant he needed it as soon as his pieces and tools arrived.

They *did* have some talking and sorting out to do.

Chapter Five

As soon as she heard the shower running, Sienna grabbed an old rag from the storeroom and hurried back into the studio to wipe up the coffee on the floor before going back out to the gallery.

She groaned. She'd seen the big road bike parked beneath the tree up the street before she drove her car around the corner to the small parking lot at the back of the gallery but hadn't given a thought to it being Jack's. She'd planned to work on the next batch of frogs for her show all day, and now her plans had been thrown into disarray with his arrival. Her show was only three weekends away, and managing the gallery took up most of her time. Now Jack would slow her down even more. Meeting with him, showing him around and seeing exactly what he wanted her role to be—if indeed she still had a job, let alone an exhibition—was going to take up time. Assuming he would come by when the shop was open had been stupid. He *was* the gallery owner. He could come in any time he liked. And it looked like he was planning on staying here, too.

Of course he'd come in on the weekend.

She just hadn't expected him to be here this morning. All she could hope was that bunking here was a temporary arrangement, because it would interfere with her preparation for her exhibition until she could find another studio to work in. She looked around with a sigh. It had taken her an entire week to move her equipment and pieces from Mountain View, and she wasn't looking forward to moving it all again. And the kilns downstairs were perfect for her work.

Why would a businessman from Melbourne even want to own an art gallery in Queensland? Products, he'd said!

She tried to remember what Ana had told her about Jack when he'd come down for Faith's christening last year. All she could remember was that he didn't work in the same company Blake had, and that he had a reputation for liking a good time.

Because his family was loaded.

Last year at the christening, they'd indulged in a bit of flirting at Ana's cottage, but he'd left before dinner. And she hadn't seen him again until he'd walked into Fish Divine last night.

He'd looked good then, and he looked even better this morning. His hair was rumpled, and the dark stubble on his jaw tempted her fingers. She'd dropped her gaze to a muscled bare chest and refused to acknowledge the little flip low in her tummy. Closing her eyes, Sienna recalled the cheeky grin on his face as he'd zipped his jeans over the black boxers she saw before looking away. She remembered the first time she'd seen him up in Maleny a couple of years back. She'd told Ana two gorgeous guys were in the store and sent Georgie a text message about sex on legs or something.

Well, he certainly was that, and she was going to have to forget it until she found out what his intentions were for the gallery. Her exhibition was booked, and all the flyers were about to go up all over town. Noosa Heads was ready for her show.

I have to be ready too.

Chapter Six

Giovanni's Café was the best eatery in the area; Sienna was a regular customer. She had an appointment with them tomorrow to go over catering for her launch.

"Just a black coffee, thanks, Sophie."

Sienna glanced up at the waitress who stood between them, waiting for Jack to finish looking at the menu. Once he'd come out of the bathroom, showered, and dressed in jeans and a T-shirt, she led him down Hastings Street to her favourite coffee shop. Now Sophie was ogling Jack and the broad shoulders beneath his T-shirt. Sienna tried to ignore the tight shirt moulded to his shoulders and chest, and the way his hair flopped onto his forehead when he'd wandered out to the gallery after his shower. The smell of the citrus aftershave that wafted over her when she'd locked the front door of the gallery hadn't helped, either.

Ignore it. Jack is my boss. This is a professional relationship.

"Pancakes, bacon, and fried eggs." He grinned up at Sophie, and Sienna could swear the girl was turning to jelly as she took the order. He was so happy and carefree, as though he didn't have a worry in the world.

Okay, so he's easy on the eye. I'll admit that. And he's got a sexy voice.

"Coffee?" Sophie held his gaze and he nodded before he glanced at Sienna.

"You're not eating?" he asked.

"No, just coffee for me." She glanced down at her watch and frowned. Her stomach was in knots—there was no way she could eat until she knew what was going to happen. "As soon as our meeting is done, I need to get back to the studio. I have a lot of work planned for today."

Jack nodded, and the waitress headed to the kitchen. Sienna followed his gaze as he looked around the small courtyard that was located at the side of the shop. There were only two other customers there so early in the day. Old wooden wine casks were scattered among the tables and on either side of the doors, filled with the last of the summer flowers. Asters, zinnias, and dahlias spilled over the edges of the wooden tubs in a profusion of colours. The paving was weathered and covered with moss in the shaded corners. In the distance, the sound of the surf added to the relaxing atmosphere.

The low rumble of Jack's sexy voice drew her attention back from the flowers and to her current problem. "This is a pretty place. Very trendy," he said. "And there are a lot of galleries in the shopping area. I didn't know there were so many here."

So he didn't know much about the place.

"What made you decide to buy the gallery?" Her voice was short, and Sienna studied him while she waited for him to answer.

Jack put his elbows on the table and linked his fingers beneath his chin. "Promise not to laugh?"

"Not until I hear what you have to say."

"I'm a movie fanatic. I bought the gallery because so many movie stars live here on the coast."

"What? Where did you hear that?" Sienna felt her mouth drop open. She closed it and reached for the coffee Sophie put on the table.

'I think you've got Noosa confused with Byron Bay.'

"He put his hands up. "No, just joking. I've always been interested in art, so I decided to buy a gallery and host exhibitions. Noosa seemed as good a place as any. A wealthy, retired clientele who are looking to build up their art collections live here." He stared into the distance and Sienna sensed there was more to the story. She wasn't going to press him. It wasn't his past she was interested in; it was *her* future.

"I saw Sea View Gallery in one of the art magazines I subscribe to."

"So you bought it, had it managed, and then you decided to sell it a couple of months ago? And then you changed your mind again." Sienna frowned. It sounded as though Jack didn't know what he wanted. Her entire future was at stake because a flirty playboy with time on his hands and money to burn bought a gallery he didn't even seem much interested in. "And now you're going to take it over?"

Buy. Sell. Keep. Move in. Why would he do that? It was the bottom line that mattered. All *his* choices were affecting *her* plans.

Jack leaned back casually and put his hands behind his head, turning his face up to the sunshine that had begun to bathe the courtyard. "I thought I'd be in Melbourne for good after my dad got sick, but, well…here I am." The corded muscles in his neck and his toned biceps didn't look they belonged to a businessman, but more like the gym junkie she'd first mistaken him for. Now Sienna stared at him, waiting for him to keep talking and spill his plans for the gallery.

"Look, there's been a mix-up. I'm sorry. I'll have to call Dad's secretary. I told her to take the gallery off the market when I—"

She waited for Jack to continue, but he cut off his sentence. After a couple of minutes of silence, she couldn't wait any longer. "We need to sort out what's happened, and you need to tell me what you are going to do."

Jack nodded. "We do. And soon."

"How about now? I have to make plans." Sienna fought her rising temper. "Perhaps I was a bit hasty making plans before the sale was final. I have my first exhibition opening in three weeks. I had no idea you would change your mind. In fact, remember, I didn't even know it was you selling to me."

"Would that have made a difference if you had?" Jack narrowed his eyes.

"Why would it? I barely know you." Sienna waved her hand dismissively. "I haven't given you another thought since you took my number."

Liar.

She had, and she still remembered how disappointed she'd been when he left Faith's christening early, and then never called her. Despite what she'd said to Georgie, there was still a place in her life for going out with men and having a good time. Just because she didn't want the commitment-and-wedding deal like Georgie didn't mean she was going to live a nun's life. She'd just been too busy to go out, building up the gallery's business and her reputation as an artist. And now Jack had to turn up and own the damn gallery. Too complicated.

"Until last night I thought the contract of sale would go ahead. I've made plans, and, yes, maybe I was a bit premature, but I'm not known for being patient." Sienna put her cup down and folded her arms across her chest. "If I had known this was going to happen, I would have stayed at Mountain View Gallery."

"So you haven't been at my gallery for very long?"

Sienna shook her head and gritted her teeth. *His* gallery. God, he didn't even know what was happening before he waltzed in to take over. Was he serious about the business? She couldn't work for someone with such a casual attitude. Sienna needed to be organised, and everything she did was planned ahead.

"I've only been there a couple of months. My…your…gallery had been closed for a few months after the other manager left town. You didn't even know that?" She tried to keep her voice even. No point upsetting him although she'd probably done that already.

Jack shrugged and a frown wrinkled his brow. For the first time he seemed a little uncomfortable. "No…no, I'm sorry, but I had no idea. I have a lot of business interests that Dad's company looks after for me. Maybe I should have paid more attention." He leaned back as Sophie put a plate overflowing with food in front of him. It seemed as though the discomfort she had glimpsed a moment ago disappeared. "Looks great, thanks."

Sienna sat back and watched Jack dig into the meal, as she weighed the pros and cons of what her choices were. Her stomach grumbled, and he grinned at her as the heat warmed her neck.

"You should eat something. You're too thin."

Now her temper really began to boil. "I eat plenty. I'm petite, not thin."

"What did you have for breakfast?"

She pointed to her coffee.

Jack sighed and used his fork to lift a pancake and a slice of bacon onto the small plate that held his toast. He slid it over to her. "Eat. We have a lot of talking to do."

"Thank you." Sienna nibbled at the edge of the pancake and stared at him. "So start."

"Start what?"

God, he was laidback. She spoke through her teeth with forced restraint. "Start talking."

He grinned and kept eating without saying a word, until his plate was clear. "That was great." Finally, he picked up the napkin and wiped his mouth. "Okay, tell me what *your* plans are."

"You're the owner. You tell me." Sienna kept her voice patient and held his gaze.

"But *you* did have plans?" Jack's green eyes crinkled when he smiled, and her stomach did a little flip.

Hunger and not enough coffee.

She caught Sophie's eye when the waitress walked past and pointed to her empty cup.

"Well, yes, I did. Like I said, I like to know what's ahead, and I plan for it. This has thrown me a curveball, and I need to rethink where I am…and where I'll go."

"Maybe you don't have to go anywhere." Jack leaned forward and propped his elbows on the table as he held her gaze.

"I need to know…are you going to be hands-on, or are you going to be an owner who only comes in occasionally?"

Jack stared back at her, and his eyes were full of mirth. "Definitely not hands-on, not in the gallery anyway."

The subtext in his words was clear by the grin on his face. Despite the pleasant shiver that ran down Sienna's back, she gritted her teeth to hold back a rude retort. He was trying to push her buttons. Why did he take it off the market if he didn't want to work in it?

"So you'll support any exhibitions I've already booked, including mine?"

"Yours?"

God, the man was casual.

"Yes, I told you before. I'm an artist. I'm planning my first show at the end of the month." She spoke slowly as she stared at him. "And I have advertised it, so I need to know right away if I need to find another gallery, seeing as I won't have my own now."

Jack returned her stare. "You're a bit out of sorts this morning."

Finally, she was getting through to him.

"This is me. I like to be organised." She forced a smile to her face, and it was at odds with the temper she was barely hanging on to. "I need to know what you're going to do. It might be hard for someone as…for someone like you to understand, but this is my livelihood." She couldn't help herself and her temper finally spilled over. "Anyone who buys a gallery because they think movie stars live in town, and then leaves it in the hands of a manager who leaves and he doesn't even know it sits there all closed up—"

"Whoa...right there." Jack held his hand up again. "You've got yourself all worked up. Look, I'm sorry the sale fell through, but I have my reasons. And what do you mean by someone like me?"

She pursed her lips, arms still folded. "Nothing." She'd been forthright enough already. "Okay, my plans...if you are happy for the first exhibition—mine—to go ahead, I need three things to happen."

"Okay. Tell me."

"One. Do you need a manager, someone to do the day-to-day gallery stuff?"

He held her gaze and nodded without speaking.

"Two, can I still hold my exhibition in the gallery the week I've advertised?"

"Yes." He nodded again as relief flooded through Sienna. Now his arms were folded across his chest. "And three?"

So far, so good.

This was the one she really needed him to agree to. There was no way Sienna could move her stuff to another studio and have her pieces ready in time. And there was no formal agreement in her employment contract for the manager to use the studio. She swallowed and her fingers bit into the skin on her arms.

"Three, can I keep using the studio?"

"No."

Chapter Seven

Jack looked across the table at Sienna. The twin spots of colour were back on her cheeks, and he could tell she was about to lose her cool. Beneath the table she was tapping her foot against the cobblestones.

"I'm going to stay in the studio until I find somewhere permanent to live, so you'll have to find somewhere else to work." He leaned back in his chair. He wasn't ready to tell her that he planned to use it for his work, too.

Not just yet.

He was still trying to figure her out, and he wasn't ready to share his private work with her. When they had first met, he'd thought she was a little distant because she was being protective of Ana, and he'd admired that.

She shrugged. "Can't do."

"Can't do what?" Now her attitude was starting to get under his skin.

"If I have to move to another studio, I won't be ready for the show. And I certainly wouldn't have the time to manage the gallery for you. So, we have a catch-22."

"Maybe we'll have to look for a compromise?" The last thing Jack wanted was to have to manage the gallery himself, and he didn't want to have to find a new manager. It wouldn't be a good look for the business to close the place again so soon after it had been shut for a few months. He needed to keep Sienna in place as manager. Maybe he could postpone his work on his own pieces for a couple of weeks. If she would stay, maybe he could give a little. "What if you could use the studio for the next two weeks and then find somewhere else after that?" He could afford to give her two weeks, but that was all.

"Two weeks. I could possibly do that. Any other conditions attached? Like a rental fee?"

"God, no. You can just use the space. As long as there's room for me to store my stuff somewhere when it arrives, and you can work around it."

"How much stuff?" She tapped her finger against her lips.

He hadn't noticed her hands before. Her nails were short and square cut and didn't match the rest of her flamboyant style. Long, painted nails would match the colourful scarves and the dangling earrings. *But she is an artist*. So that explained the functional look of her hands.

"A lot."

"How long were you planning on living in the studio? I can't work if you're sleeping there."

"That's true. That could be a problem." Jack frowned. He wasn't ready to find a place of his own here yet. He rubbed the back of his neck. He didn't want to let her down, but things were getting complicated now.

"The sooner you find somewhere to live, the sooner I can get back to work." Sienna kept her fingers against her lips as she looked at him thoughtfully. "There's a real shortage of rentals here in Noosa…and it's really expensive. You might have to move to a hotel."

Jack bit back the niggle of temper that tugged at him. She might like to be organised and call the shots, but there was no way she was going to send him to a hotel when he owned a perfectly good studio to sleep in. He kept his voice even. "I hate hotel living."

"Even for two weeks?"

"Even for one night. It's not an option I'd consider."

Sienna stared at him and frowned. Her fingers drummed on the table, and she held his gaze. Her expression changed, and a slight smile tipped her lips. Jack looked at her mouth and was surprised by the rush of feeling that ran through him. She looked at him thoughtfully.

"I might have a solution. I have a proposition for you." Her smile was wider.

The thoughts running through Jack's mind had nothing to do with where he was going to live, and he forced himself to concentrate on what she was saying.

"There's a small apartment in the back of my cottage. Near the lake. You could have that until you find something better. You could move in today, and I could keep working in the studio. Two weeks. What do you think?" Her eyes were wide and her expression hopeful. His return to take over the gallery had really put a hole in her plans.

"I'll take a look at it and think about it." He didn't know how interested he was in her offer. Sure, he could see she'd only offered because it meant she could get back into the studio. But as far as working with her in the gallery, and living in her house…well, he didn't know how he felt about that. He wanted to date her, but living and working in the same place? That was a bit too much.

"How about we go now and you can look at it? Then I can get to work as soon as we get back."

A strong desire to reach across the table and put his hand around the back of her long, slender neck and pull Sienna to him so he could kiss those lips overtook him.

Whoa, not yet. Let's get the first problem sorted out.

"Okay. Won't hurt to take a look." Jack knew his voice was gruff, but he was fighting the feelings tugging him back and forward. He stood, pushed his chair in, and walked across the courtyard to the cash register. He'd check out this apartment of hers, but it would be better if he found a place of his own. Maybe he'd make some calls after he looked at it and see if he could find somewhere else to live for a while.

And quickly.

He needed somewhere he could have his own space—somewhere to put her at a distance. Jack needed privacy and solitude for the muse to kick in. And he couldn't afford to risk it—his deadline was fast approaching. He didn't want anything to dent his confidence; God knows, Dad had a big enough go at doing that. Living in close proximity to Sienna would complicate matters even more, and if there was one thing he didn't want, it was to make it hard to focus on his sculptures because his head was somewhere else. He'd been living with his parents since his father's heart attack and was more than ready to live alone again.

That was just *one* of the reasons he wasn't too keen on taking up Sienna's offer. The other one was that she was just too damn appealing, and he didn't want to put himself near her just yet. They had to keep a professional relationship now that they would be working closely together. Sex complicated matters. He'd been down that road before…and more than once. His last girlfriend had read him wrong, and Arielle had mapped out a whole future for them before he'd pulled back. He wasn't going to risk it again, especially when they had this business connection. If it were just a fun relationship, they could move on—with mutual agreement—when it burned out. Jack wanted no complications; having the gallery connection would complicate matters. Let alone living in the same place. Twenty-four-seven. No way.

"Come on, we'll take my car." She strode ahead of him, and he was surprised by how quickly she moved. Sienna barely reached his shoulder, but he had to step up his pace to catch her.

The streets had filled with tourists and locals alike since they'd been in the coffee shop, and he looked around with interest. Sienna slowed down and shot him a grin. "Looking for movie stars?"

It was the same droll humour that had appealed to him when they'd first met.

"Nah, just checking out my new town." The place had a fresh feel. After his time in the hectic world of business in Melbourne, he was looking forward to the change. A relaxed lifestyle. A slower pace. A place where integrity and honesty could exist without someone trying to make money from his hard work. Or better him in a deal.

She walked along beside him. "You know *anybody* you pass on the street could be a *somebody* here. But there is a code of anonymity in Noosa. Even if you pass Chris Hemsworth…you just keep on walkin'."

"I'm sure." If he saw Chris Hemsworth, he'd probably gawk like a fan.

"I'll teach you the Noosa way." She'd relaxed a bit, probably because of the possibility of getting her workspace back, and that made him uncomfortable. He felt as though she was happy because things might work out her way, not because she was enjoying his company. He was sure if it hadn't meant being able to stay working in the studio, she would never have offered to show him the apartment. She kept walking past the gallery, then turned into a back lane.

"You keep your car back here?" he asked.

"Yes, there's just enough space for it."

Sienna walked over to a red BMW Z3 parked in a small paved area and leaned over to unlock the door. Jack felt that small tug of desire pull at him again as her loose pants clung to her legs. He lifted his gaze and ran it down the car instead. "Nice car."

"I love it," she said with a smile. "Especially when I drive back up the mountain to visit Georgie and Ana, and the weather's good enough to keep the top down."

'Which lake do you live near?'

'Lake Weyba. It's only a short drive from here.'

He opened the passenger door, slid in next to her, and watched as she reached up and pushed the front part of the top up, before turning the key and pressing the electronic control to open the roof. It slid back silently, and they were bathed in warm sunshine.

"Almost as good as riding a bike," he said.

"Might as well enjoy the day. Sunny days can be few and far between here along this stretch of the coast."

The wind blew strongly as Sienna drove out through town and took the turnoff at Noosaville. Jack dropped his shades over his eyes when they turned south. He took in the scenery and recognised the golf course where he'd played with Blake a couple of years ago. When they passed Noosa Hills, Sienna swung a right onto Eumarella Road. "Pretty exclusive area," he said.

"The average listing is over two million," she said.

Jack narrowed his gaze. She must be doing okay if she had a place here *and* was going to buy the gallery too. Maybe she could find herself another studio and he wouldn't feel so bad about moving her out.

"You are easy to read, you know." Sienna turned and grinned at him as she swung into a driveway and drove past a huge home between some tall pines. "I said the average." He appreciated her smile; she'd looked thoughtful as they'd driven through town and hadn't said much to him.

She slowed in front of a huge house built in pink concrete, with large circular windows on each side of a tall entry that towered over an expanse of green manicured lawn. He waited for Sienna to turn into the circular driveway at the front, but she kept going. A little farther down the road, the lake glimmered through the trees and she swung left into a narrow driveway. A small cottage sat on a rise at the end of the road with a garage beside it.

"Home sweet home." She stopped in front of the cottage and turned the car off.

"Nice." Jack let out a low whistle when he stepped out and took in the view of the lake. "Very nice. Lived here long?" It was exactly the sort of place he'd love to find down here along the coast. He'd thought of having ocean views, but this small lake, hidden among the trees, was beautiful.

"When I was first working with Georgie and Ana in our restoration business, it was one of the first old places we bought. It used to be the boat cottage of the estate up the road. It was going for a song because it was in such poor condition." Sienna walked up the three steps, and Jack followed her to the porch. "We pooled what we had and it was our first restoration."

The view was even better from the porch. The cottage was so far from the road there was no traffic noise. Jack closed his eyes and listened to the wind sighing through the trees.

He could move in here right now. His fingers tingled with the urge to get working.

"Local gossip says the estate once belonged to an American movie star, and this was his love cottage." She grinned at him and her face came alive. "We learned a lot doing the renovation. And we had so much fun. Because it was so far from Maleny, we'd stay overnight, camping in the forest." She pointed to a low fence with a gate at the side of the cottage. "When we finished the restoration, we rented it out, and then when we closed the business, I bought the girls' share and I moved down here last year." She put the key in the front door and led him through the small cottage. "The only downside to the apartment is that it shares a common entry with the house. That's why I haven't rented it out before. It's got everything else, but it's really tiny."

"Show me." As he followed her down a wide timber-lined hallway, Jack watched her walk. Her movements were graceful, and he regretted not having the opportunity to follow up that promise of calling her.

Too late now, especially if he was going to be her boss…and her tenant.

Chapter Eight

"So, what do you think?"

Jack stood at the window of the small living room. The apartment at the back of the cottage had an uninterrupted view of the lake. Sienna smiled to herself. There hadn't been any view until she, Ana, and Georgie had cleared the overgrown garden. The house and its garden were one of the best restorations they'd done. That's why they never sold it.

"This light is amazing."

She jumped when Jack turned to her, his face alight with enthusiasm. "Have you ever thought of adding a studio to the back here? The aspect is perfect."

"I did, but I can't afford it." She looked at him thoughtfully. "I saved everything to buy a gallery, but that's not such a bad idea. Now that the sale's not going ahead."

"Have you ever thought about selling?"

"The apartment?" She tipped her head to the side, unsure of what he was saying.

"No, the whole property." His eyes were bright with interest, and he came over and held her arms gently. Sienna tried to ignore the jolt of warmth that shot up her shoulders and settled in her chest when his fingers brushed down her arms before stopping at her wrists.

"Maybe we could do a deal with the gallery?"

She bit back her frustration at his attitude. She had so wanted that gallery for her own; Jack had it and didn't really want it. And now he wanted her house, too?

"Uh-uh. I'm settled here." She kept her voice bland.

He stared down at her and the warmth fluttered to her stomach. His gaze held hers, and she let go of a little of her anger. How could she not when that sexy grin homed in on her?

"Well, give me some thought if you ever do decide to sell it."

"I guess this means you'll take the apartment…for the two weeks anyway, while I get my exhibition ready?" She tried to steer the conversation back to their original problem and ignore the crazy feelings racing through her from where his fingers were touching her skin.

"Yeah, but you can only have the studio for two weeks. Do you think you could be ready by then?"

She looked at him thoughtfully and tapped her finger to her lips. "Maybe."

"You have to."

Sienna looked at him. He had let go of her and had an intense look on his face. He was flexing his fingers as he walked around. "Okay. If I work every night, I can do it in two."

Jack stopped in front of her and held his hand out. "We have a deal then."

Sienna took a deep breath and took his hand as relief zinged through her.

Maybe this will work out okay. After all, Jack owed her nothing really, and he *was* letting her have the studio in town and hold her exhibition. The only thing in it for him was having someone to manage the gallery for him just like she'd been doing already.

"Come on. I'll show you the garage. There's room in there if you want to store your stuff when it arrives." Sienna stepped away from his loose hold and headed back through the house and out onto the porch, conscious of him close behind her. God, she was acting like a teenager. She'd never let a man affect her like that before, and she wasn't about to start now. Men had a role in her life. She went on dates, she had the occasional fling, and she didn't let any of them close enough to hurt her. She swallowed and straightened her shoulders.

And I won't now. I'm not Georgie.

Between Georgie and their mother, there was enough hurt to last them all a lifetime. Sienna didn't intend on adding to it.

"In here," she said briskly as she opened the swinging wooden doors to the empty garage. "Can you fit all your stuff in here?"

Jack walked in, his thumbs tucked into his jeans, and looked around. "It'll be fine. I'll put my personal stuff here and the big stuff can go into the space at the back of the gallery."

He must be planning on storing his furniture too.

Sienna didn't care what he put in there as long as it meant she could use the studio. She went inside to get the spare key to the front door and the padlock for the garage, while Jack walked over and waited by the car.

God, she hoped she wasn't making a huge mistake. Working with him and living in the same house meant she would have to try twice as hard to keep him at a distance. She'd had a lot of practice being tough, and she was about to invoke it now. That soft feeling that had crept through her bones earlier was banished to a place she never let see the light of day. She hadn't been out with anyone for a while. She'd have the same reaction to any good-looking guy who came along.

Yeah, sure.

The little voice in her head let the doubts creep in. It had been in the back of her mind since she'd first met Jack, and now the attraction whooshed straight back in with a vengeance.

As soon as they got back to the gallery, Jack packed up his bag, ready to head out to the apartment. He said he had some calls to make to get the delivery address for his gear changed. Sienna drew a deep breath of relief when he finally roared off on his bike. Her mind was in turmoil, and she needed to get into the studio and do what she loved.

And figure out what I'm going to do. How to fit the gallery in through the day and get four weeks' worth of work done in two. She couldn't understand why he would only give her the two weeks? Maybe he was just being ornery and had to show her who was the boss? But that didn't fit what she'd seen of Jack's casual character.

Sienna lifted a drop sheet and picked up a plastic crate full of her copper frogs. They were shaped and ready for enamelling. She lifted the roller door at the back of the gallery and walked down the ramp to the bricked-in room beneath, and she wondered if Jack knew the room with the kilns was there.

Sienna shrugged and tried to clear her mind as she fired the kiln and reached for a small container of ground enamel.

***

Jack unpacked the panniers and the one bag he'd carried on the bike from Melbourne before he made his calls. He really needed to harness the ideas that were flowing through him. He pulled out a notebook and did a couple of quick sketches of the pictures in his mind before he lost them. Then he called the moving company, and now he was calling home to check on his father. As the phone rang, he looked around the small apartment. Every colour and every piece of furniture reminded him of Sienna—her vibrancy. It would be a good place to chill while he thought about the work ahead of him.

"Hey, Jack!" His dad's voice boomed across the connection. "Great to hear from you, son." Jack grinned. At least having a life-threatening heart attack had given Mike Montgomery a whole new perspective on life. They'd fought for years, about how Jack didn't want to work in the family business, and his mother, Helen, was caught in the middle. His laid-back attitude really got under his workaholic father's skin. Life was too short, and his father had finally realised that point with his heart attack. It had given him a huge wake-up call.

"How are you, Dad?"

"All good. Can't talk long. I'm getting picked up for golf in a minute."

"Mum there?"

"No, she's at the office."

"On a Sunday?" Jack frowned. He hoped his mother wasn't going to step into the shoes his father had vacated.

"Yeah, the sooner Blake gets up here the better." His father cleared his throat. "Uh-oh, scratch that. I wasn't supposed to say anything."

"Blake?"

"He'll tell you what's happening. Forget I said anything. How's that deadline looking?"

Jack bit back a terse reply. "Fine, fine. Remember I only arrived here last night." He hated the fact that he felt it necessary to make excuses to his father.

After he disconnected the call, Jack walked thoughtfully into the small bedroom. Sienna had told him where to find some sheets, and after he'd made up the bed, he lay back with his hands behind his head, going over the events of the day. Nothing had really panned out like he'd expected, but that was the way he liked life to be. He wasn't going to get trapped on the treadmill of predictability where he always knew what the day would bring, with too many people depending on him. Look what it had done to his father. Although when he'd been in Melbourne, his own need to control what was happening in the company had surfaced a little and unsettled him. He worried he had more of his father in him than he thought. Maybe that's why they clashed for so long.

So once he'd signed the contract for the sculptures, he'd hightailed it out of the business and out of the city. Now he'd have all day to work on his sculpture, focus his creativity, and do what he loved. The only small problem was the deadline on the contract he'd signed, but that didn't bother him as much as not being able to work for two weeks. In a way, he already regretted saying Sienna could use the studio. He would have to be firm and stick to the timeline he'd given her. Then he'd move in there, finish his commissions, and start work on the ideas crowding his thoughts.

When he had more done, he could think about his own exhibition.

As long as Sienna would keep managing the gallery.

If she was happy to stay at the gallery after her exhibition, that was fine. If she did choose to move on, he'd have to deal with it. And he wasn't going to complicate matters with a personal relationship. As much as he would have liked to start up something between them, things had to stay on a business footing.

He closed his eyes and frowned as her face continued to fill his thoughts. He rolled over and punched the pillow. This had to stop. He focused on where he would get the truck to deliver his stuff. He'd have to split it when it arrived and decide what would go where.

It'd be crazy to move even one sculpture twice, but it had put a dent in his plans having to wait a couple of weeks before he could start work. There was enough space and light here to do some of his modelling, but he needed the kilns, so he'd wait out the two weeks. He ignored the little voice telling him that he was worried his work wouldn't measure up.

But he'd made a deal with Sienna and he'd stick to his word. He wouldn't let being at loose ends interfere with his decision to keep her at arm's length. If he got bored just hanging around and not working, he'd go out and explore the district. Go up and visit Blake.

Play some golf. Catch a wave. He'd leave Sienna in peace until she'd finished her own work, and then he'd get to know about the gallery when she wasn't so busy.

The problem was that wasn't the way his thoughts were taking him. Finally, he drifted off and awoke refreshed a short time later. The afternoon stretched ahead, and Jack decided to go for a walk around the lake. When he opened the front door, he noticed the *Noosa News* lying on the table on the porch, and he tucked it beneath his arm as he set off.

***

By the time Sienna finished enamelling the batch of frogs, it was after dark. She pushed her helmet up and rubbed her eyes. It was hot down here with the kilns on, and her clothes were damp from perspiration. Her stomach was grumbling; she'd only snatched a quick lunch once she'd finished the first batch of frogs and hadn't eaten since. As soon as she got home, a shower, a meal, and a glass of wine on her back porch would complete the day. She put her hand up to her eyes and rubbed.

She arranged the frogs on the shelves and stood back. Satisfaction rippled through her.

They were good. In fact, they were better than good.

They're fabulous. If I say so myself.

The red one with his leg dangling inches below the green enamelled log she'd wrapped him around was her favourite. It was one of the best pieces she'd done yet. Three more batches to enamel and she'd be ready for the show. But tomorrow she had planned to focus on publicity and organising event logistics. There weren't enough hours to get everything done. She had some more media sheets to send out, and she had back-to-back appointments with artists wanting to book their own shows, as well as meeting with the caterers for her first-night launch event.

Where will Jack fit into all this?

Even though they discussed the studio and his living arrangements, they hadn't discussed anything about her day-to-day running of the gallery now that he was here. He was so casual about it. Did he really want the gallery to succeed or not? She shrugged, flicked on the night-light to leave the gallery softly lit, and pulled the door shut behind her.

She'd keep doing things her way until he told her to change them.

Fifteen minutes later, she drove her sports car into the small carport next to her cottage. The house was in darkness, although she noticed that the padlock on the garage doors was locked. Jack was likely home and in bed already. Sienna let herself in quietly, slipped off her shoes and padded barefoot along to her bathroom. She threw her clothes into the linen basket and turned the shower on hot. The hard jets of water soothed her neck and refreshed her, and once she was dry, she tucked a towel around her breasts and wandered into her bedroom. Maybe it hadn't been such a good idea, jumping in and offering him the apartment. It was going to be hard getting used to having someone else around. No more wandering around half dressed. She slipped on some underwear and tied a loose sarong around her before she headed out to the kitchen.

It won't be for long.

Once she finished the last batch of firing in the kiln in two weeks, she could start looking for a studio. Then she had to decide whether she was going to stay working for him or look for some other place to buy. She bit her lip. Jack's idea about building a studio on the back of the cottage had given her something to think about. If she stayed managing his gallery, and could work on her sculptures from home, it could be the ideal solution. She just had to find the money to do it.

His decision to take the gallery off the market had created a lot of problems for her. Her thoughts whirled around as she made a grilled cheese sandwich and poured a glass of wine. Maybe, just maybe, she could build herself a studio out here on the lake. Using her shoulder to push open the back door, she headed out to the porch.

"You're home late."

Sienna jumped and grabbed for the plate before it slipped from her hand. Jack unfolded himself from her hammock, crossed the porch, and took the plate from her.

She put her hand on her chest as her heart thudded. "You scared me. I'm not used to company."

"Sorry. I was sitting out here enjoying the quiet." He pulled out a chair and put her plate on the table. "You don't eat properly."

Sienna bit down on the smart retort that hovered on her lips and forced a smile in his direction. He really brought out the worst in her.

What is it to him what I do or what I eat?
"I had a good lunch."
"That's okay, then."
She couldn't help herself, despite her intention to keep things non-emotional. "I'm so pleased you approve." Putting her elbows on the table, she glared at him in the soft moonlight. She'd left the outside light off deliberately to keep the insects away before she'd come outside. Despite the cool breeze, Jack was wearing running shorts and no shirt, and her reaction to the sight of his broad, muscular chest bugged her even more. She pushed away the flare of desire that sparked inside her. "Aren't you cold?"

"No, I went for a run around the lake after I ate. I miss my gym equipment. I'll have to find a place to work out around here."

Sienna reached over and picked up the small lighter she kept on the table and lit the vanilla candle in the glass bowl in the centre. She drew a deep breath and held her hand steady, surprised by the tremble his proximity caused. The candle threw a flickering light over Jack's bare skin and she caught her breath. Tipping her head back, she looked up at the stars. It was only his natural beauty that she found appealing. Her artistic eye was drawn by beauty.

Nothing else.

She dropped her head and looked out over the lake shimmering in the moonlight. The low branches of the trees surrounding the cottage bowed elegantly in the light breeze, their leaves forming long, draping sweeps illuminated by the soft light.

"It's beautiful here." Jack's voice was a whisper, and a shiver snaked up her spine.

Maybe she should do something about this feeling? Let this attraction run its course? What did they say about only living once?

Not worth the risk.

"Yes, it is."

"Did you get your work done? You put in a long day."

Pleased to get her mind off the bare, muscular shoulders across the table, Sienna nodded. "Yes, I got a good amount done. I should be able to finish in the two weeks if I put in the next couple of weekends as well as every night."

"Do you always work this hard?"

She nodded. "Not usually every night. But what has to be done, will be. And I love my work. I lose myself in it." She looked up at him. Maybe it would be hard for a businessman—and one with such a casual attitude—to understand what she was saying about the creative process.

"Where do you do your enamelling?" Jack held her gaze steadily with his. He seemed genuinely interested, so she kept talking.

She looked back at him. "Did you look at my frogs in the gallery today?"

All Sienna's confidence in her work faded in that instant and she bit her lip. Then her temper kicked at the thought of Jack looking at them without her. Her mood seesawed back and forth. "Frogs? No, I read about your upcoming exhibition in the local paper."

"Oh. I forgot about that."

"According to the journalist, you're quite the up-and-coming artist in the area…and you work in enamel?"

"They say the same thing about everyone they interview."

"Tell me about your work. About the processes you use. Do the kilns beneath the gallery work?" Sienna was surprised at his level of interest and his knowledge of the process.

"I wondered if you knew there was a brick room beneath the gallery. I use those kilns." She shook her head. "You really didn't know what you bought, did you?"

Jack certainly wasn't a hands-on manager, and if that was the way he worked maybe she would be able to stay at the gallery with him as owner. He could let her run it the way she wanted and keep out of her way. As long as Jack found somewhere to live, maybe life could go on the way it was. It would just mean the gallery wouldn't belong to her, but that wouldn't be the end of the world. The money she'd set aside for the deposit could go toward adding on to her house and building her own studio, while she continued to work in the studio at the gallery. For the life of her, she couldn't understand why he wanted it. If he wasn't going to be involved, what was he going to do with his days?

"I really liked the feel of the town. Before I even ran the numbers, I decided to buy it."

The opposite of her. Sienna had everything planned down to the last detail in all her life. Jack grinned at her, and the flickering candlelight played over his bare chest.

This is altogether too romantic a setting out here. She needed to break the mood. If she was going to run his gallery, she needed to know a little bit more about the direction he wanted to go.

"What sort of art do you enjoy?"

"Oh, I have eclectic tastes. I have a few contemporary paintings in my apartment in Melbourne. Some are being shipped out, and some I'll leave there till I find a place to live. I often spend my weekends cruising galleries."

Sienna finished her wine and put the glass down. How nice would it be to be able to afford to collect art? And to have the time to wander around the galleries? When she got the chance—and that was not very often—she loved visiting art museums and other galleries. Maybe they did have something in common after all? She pushed that thought away. There'd be no sparks crackling around the table tonight if she had any say in the matter. She couldn't help but grin when she remembered last night. There was no Georgie here with family stories to dispel the tension tonight.

"Great." Jack was staring at her, and she dropped her gaze as she stood and pushed her chair back. "You found everything you needed? I'm going to bed. We've got a busy day ahead of us in the gallery tomorrow. We'll have to spend some time sorting out my role now that you've arrived."

He stood and followed her to the door, and as she turned to say good night, he held her arm. The heat running up her skin rivalled the heat of the kiln this afternoon.

"I meant to tell you; your phone rang a few times tonight." Jack looked down at her and held her gaze.

"Thanks." Sienna moved away and pushed the door open, turning the light on before she crossed to the phone. Three missed calls from Ana flashed on the screen.

All from the same number. "It's Ana. I wonder why she didn't call my cell?"

Jack grinned at her. "Maybe because you left it at home? I could hear it ringing from the front of the cottage."

"I can be a bit forgetful when I'm immersed in my work." Sienna pulled a face at him as she glanced down at her watch. "I didn't realise I'd left it here."

It was late, but she wouldn't sleep until she knew what was wrong. She pressed the return call button. "And she hasn't left any messages."

Ana's phone rang for a while and Sienna waited to leave a message, but Ana finally picked up.

"Hi, Sienna. Sorry, I was just putting Faith down. Little miss hates going to bed."

"What's wrong? Jack said you tried to call all afternoon."

"Jack?"

"Yeah, he's staying here for a while."

"Ooh-la-la. You didn't waste any time picking up where you left off."

"No, *la la*. And there was nothing to leave off, anyway." Sienna kept her voice low and flicked a glance at Jack. He was standing, looking out over the lake, and had his back turned to her. His skin was tanned, and his smooth shoulders tapered down nicely to a narrow waist above his running shorts. She swallowed and looked away before her gaze could continue down his bare thighs. "Jack's staying here only until we sort some things out with the gallery. Now what's wrong? Why were you trying to get me?"

"I called mainly to check that you were okay."

"I'm fine. Nothing to worry about, everything's good. I'll fill you in on the weekend."

"And that's another reason I called, to remind you about Faith's birthday party in two weeks. And it's a dress-up party." Ana's giggle made Sienna smile. Ana had taken to motherhood with lots of support. As well as having Georgie and Sienna as surrogate aunties, and Thelma and Mitzi as surrogate great-aunts, little Faith had most of the elderly community of Maleny as surrogate grandparents.

"Oh, dress-up. Love it."

"It's a fairy-tale theme. Have you still got your fairy costume? Wear that. Jeannie and Rod are bringing the kids down for the party." Excitement filled Ana's voice. "You should see how excited Blake is. He's putting on the biggest party ever!"

Sienna laughed. "What about Georgie? Another chance to wear pink? I know how much she loves it."

Ana chuckled. "Did you always torment her about her red hair?"

"Sure did, and she bit every time. Don't you worry, though, she tormented me right back."

Ana's laugh ended and her voice sobered. "I was a bit worried about her today. She took a call when I was at the store this afternoon and she got really upset."

"Is that sleaze-bucket Cole bothering her?"

"No, he was at the store for the Sunday shift too. He was over talking to Blake when her phone rang. I don't know who it was, but

I'm sure she was crying. She wouldn't tell me what was going on."

"I'll call her."

"I have to go. Faith's calling me. And, Sienna, invite Jack to the party, please? Blake was going to call him, but you can pass the invitation on instead. Seeing as he's at your place." Ana's voice was full of mirth once more. "Okay?"

"Okay, I'll pass it on, but don't go getting the wrong idea."

Ana's laugh rang out as Sienna disconnected.

"Everything's fine." She hung up the phone, cleared the messages on the screen, and turned to him with a grin. "Have you got a pair of tights?"

"What? Tights?"

"You've been invited to a birthday party." Sienna put her fingers to her lips and looked him up and down. "I think you'd make a lovely Prince Charming. You remind me of the one in *Shrek*."

Sienna chuckled to herself as she headed up the hall to her room and Jack's voice followed her.

"I don't think he was the hero, though, was he?"

"No, he wasn't." She held her door and peered around before she shut it. "I'll see you in the morning. Good night, Jack."

Sienna closed the door and leaned against it for a moment. She looked at the clock beside her bed. It was too late to call Georgie, especially since she'd worked at the store today. She'd call her first thing in the morning. Sienna was wired now and not a bit tired. Crossing to the window, she slid the curtains open, sat on the wide sill, and looked out over the lake. A slight breeze ruffled the waters, and there was a smell of rain in the air.

The day had ended up turning out better than she'd expected. Now to see what the week ahead would bring.

Chapter Nine

Jack reached for the antique phone receiver on the glass counter at the front of the gallery. It was at least the tenth time he'd answered it in the past half hour. Sienna was showing some tall guy around, and they were standing at the back of the room, head to head, deep in conversation. An unfamiliar shaft of jealousy hit Jack's chest as he watched the guy loop his arm casually over Sienna's shoulder. As he answered the question on the phone, a deliveryman pushed through the front door carrying two large boxes with FRAGILE stickers plastered over them and dumped the boxes on the desk beside the phone. He shoved the electronic delivery screen in front of Jack's nose.

"Hurry up, mate. My truck's parked outside."

Jack reached for the pen and scrawled his signature, without a clue as to what was in the boxes he was signing for. All he could hope was that whatever was in them was not broken.

"I'll have to take your number and get someone to call you back. Okay?" He took down the name and number of the artist on the other end of the phone and ended the call. Then he lifted the boxes carefully and put them on the floor behind the stool at the desk. When he got up from his haunches, his eyes were level with two pairs of legs, clad in sheer black stockings. His gaze travelled higher. Similar tight black skirts, frilly shirts, and business jackets. He stood and smiled, and the shorter woman held out her hands with a warm smile.

"Welcome to Noosa. Ms. Sacchi tells us you've bought the gallery? Is she available?" The taller woman spoke with a slight European accent. "We have an appointment."

"Who?" He had no idea who she was talking about. Then it dawned on him that he didn't even know Sienna's last name. She'd always been…well…just Sienna.
"Thanks…yes, I have. Take a seat." He pointed to the curved black-and-white-striped love seat by the door. "I'll let Ms. Sacchi know you are here."

Jack walked to the back of the gallery and grinned. He felt like a secretary. How the heck did she do this by herself all day? Why wasn't there more staff?

The smooth, tall guy was standing too close to Sienna for Jack's liking, and he took great delight in interrupting them.

"Excuse me, Ms. Sacchi." He dropped the grin and put on his best business voice. "Your next appointment is waiting for you."

Sienna's head flew up and she narrowed her eyes. "Thank you. I'll be there in a moment." She took the guy's arm and turned away from Jack, and he felt summarily dismissed.

"Perhaps you'd like to offer them a drink while they wait?" He glanced back and her wide dark eyes were dancing with mischief. She knew exactly how he was feeling, and he shot her a grin.

"Of course, Ms. Sacchi. Is there anything else you'd like me to do?"

"Perhaps you could dust the shelves, and then go to the post office and get the mail?" Jack could see the smile playing around her lips.

"Of course." He nodded. "If you could just direct me to the post office?"

"It's down past the coffee shop we went to." Her face broke into an impish grin and his heart kicked up a beat as her dark eyes held his gaze a little too long before she looked away.

What the hell is going on here?

Turning back to the front of the store, Jack caught sight of his reflection in the mirrored wall behind the shelves holding an array of coloured bowls. He certainly didn't look like an art gallery assistant. His jeans had a rip in one knee, and the clean T-shirt he'd grabbed this morning stated *Less work. More golf.* He'd intended to look around the gallery and then sit down with Sienna to discuss what they were going to do, but the morning had been hectic, so he'd pitched in. And had enjoyed every minute. Jack shrugged and headed back to the two women waiting at the front of the store. After he'd offered them a drink, it was time to get out of here for a while.

***

"Who's the new hunk?"

Sienna turned to Jeremy, who'd come back to finish the lighting for her show.

"Would you believe he owns this place?"

"Get real! True?" Jeremy watched as Jack left through the front door. "Not gay, is he?" he asked hopefully.

"Don't think so." Sienna glanced at her watch. "If we're done here, I have another appointment with the caterers."

"Sure, I'll be in touch." Jeremy air-kissed both her cheeks. "I'm looking forward to finishing this job. Even more now that I've checked out the new eye candy in the gallery."

The morning had been busier than usual, and Sienna was pleased. Maybe it would give Jack a different perspective on how the place worked. She couldn't figure him out, and it was messing with her head. At least it got her mind off this morning's conversation with Georgie. Her twin had tried to hide how upset she was, but Sienna could read her like a book. She'd always been able to, and she'd protected Georgie from the time they were small.

Marjorie, their mother, had called. Somehow, she'd finally gotten wind of them selling the restoration business and had hit Georgie up for money. She knew better than to call Sienna.

"Don't…don't even think about giving her a cent." Sienna had been so angry she'd had trouble getting the words out.

"She's our mother. And she needs it."

"She's not our mother. She took off and left us with Uncle Renzo."

"I feel sorry for her. Her partner's ill and she needs the money for his operation."

"Partner number what? Six? Seven?" Sienna had swallowed and tried to inject calm into her voice. "Georgie, listen to me. How long since we last heard from her? You think about it."

There had been a long silence at the other end of the phone. "Not for a while."

"That's right. Not since Uncle Renzo sold his business and had some spare cash. When he wouldn't listen to her, she came to get us to do her dirty work. Remember? There was a *sick* partner back then too."

"I remember." Georgie's voice had broken, and Sienna tried hard not to soften.

"Where is she now?"

"She's in Sydney, but she said she's going to come up and visit."

"If she does, I'll deal with her. Now promise me you won't do anything."

"All right. I promise. Maybe we'll catch up this weekend?"

"Probably not. I've got a stack of work to do in the studio, if I want to be free the next Sunday for Faith's birthday." Sienna had tried to lighten the conversation. "Have you got your fairy dress out?"

"Ha ha."

"Ana wants us all to wear the pink set. Did she tell you?"

"Yes, she told me. I think you're all mean to me." Georgie had laughed, to Sienna's relief. She'd ended up with the red hair and they teased her about it. "So, what's happening with the gallery?"

"I'll fill you in at the party. You're not bringing that Cal sleazebag, are you?"

"It's Cole, and no, I am not bringing him." Georgie had sighed. "But I have met this other guy—"

"That was quick."

"He's—"

"I have to go to work, talk later." Sienna knew if Georgie got started on the new guy, they'd be on the phone for ages, so she ended the call. Sometimes it was hard staying strong, but Georgie was soft-hearted, and she couldn't see when someone was trying to use her. She hadn't listened to what Sienna had tried to tell her the other night. At least she'd found something else to focus her energy on besides worrying about their mother. Hopefully the new guy she'd met wasn't another user—usually, they saw Georgie's goodness and homed straight in.

Sienna shook away the thoughts and walked to the front of the store. She greeted Gina and Carla, the caterers who worked out of Giovanni's coffee shop, and they sat down to work out the details for the launch supper at her exhibition.

The morning flew by as it always did, and as the tourists hit the streets, the gallery filled, and Sienna was pleased with the sales she made. Jack didn't reappear for a couple of hours, and she looked up as he pushed the door open with his shoulder, carrying a small plastic crate full of mail, two paper bags, and two cups of coffee.

He looked around the empty gallery, moved across to the door, and locked it. "We're closed for lunch."

"Are we?" Sienna raised her eyebrows at him.

"Yes, we are. I'm the boss, remember?" He lightened the words with a big smile and put the mail on the desk before carrying the crate to the door leading to the studio. He looked over his shoulder at her before he opened the door to the studio. "I hope you like chicken."

Sienna turned the closed sign around on the front door and reluctantly followed him. "It's a shame to close now. The streets are full of tourists."

"They have to stop for lunch, too." Jack put the crate on the floor and moved the blanket from the sofa to clear a space for Sienna. "You have to eat. You run around and use up so much energy. I don't know how you do it."

Sienna sat beside him, keeping some space between them, and looked at the heart-stoppingly-gorgeous man leaning casually back on the sofa as though he didn't have a care in the world. Picking up her coffee, she looked at him over the rim of her cup. "Telling me what to do again, Jack?" She shook her head with a half-smile. "You're going to learn the hard way, and it won't be pretty."

One corner of his mouth quirked. "I'm tough. And you do work too hard."

She avoided looking at his broad shoulders and the T-shirt straining over them. He picked up one of the bags and looked inside before handing it to her.

"Thanks." She shot him a grin. "You worked hard this morning too, Mr. Assistant."

"Totally out of my work ethic." Jack took a bite of his sandwich and his gaze settled on her as he chewed. "The gallery had a good buzz, though."

Sienna dropped her gaze, ignoring the little shiver that prickled her skin, and looked inside the sandwich bag he'd handed her. "What do you mean? Out of your work ethic?"

"I saw what working too hard did to my father." She lifted her eyes to meet his and found it hard to hold his gaze. She dropped her eyes. The fluttery feelings running around her insides were something she wasn't used to *and* something she didn't like.

Hunger. It was the smell of the fresh bread doing it to her. She unwrapped the sandwich and broke off a small piece of bread and put it in her mouth. She glanced up again, and her stomach clenched as his gaze dropped to her lips and stayed there as she chewed.

Right. Enough was enough. She pushed up to her feet and stood in front of him with her hands on her hips.

***

"What's wrong?" Jack sat up straighter. "You don't like your sandwich?"

"Will you be serious for one minute?" Sienna stomped her foot, but the soft flat pump made no noise on the wooden floor. Jack put his sandwich down. He gave her his full attention before she lost her temper. She'd worked hard this morning, and he had to remember that he was the one making the most money from the gallery, her planning and hard work, and the sales she made. He must check how much his company was paying her. He'd thought of that as she'd flitted around this morning. She looked like a butterfly darting from one end of the gallery to the other, as colourful as the pieces she had so artfully arranged on the shelves. Flat black shoes and shiny leggings sat beneath a loose multi-coloured sheer top draping down to her elbows. Her feistiness, her energy, and her volatility hid how petite she actually was. Her personality was big enough to more than make up for her lack of size, and she was absolutely beautiful.

"Stop gawking at me. It makes me uncomfortable." She glared at him, and those spots of colour appeared high on her cheeks again. Her dark eyes glittered.

"Sorry." He hadn't meant to make her uncomfortable, but he *was* enjoying the view. "Did I ever tell you that you remind me of my Aunt Caroline?"

"No." She frowned, wondering what he was going to say.

"She's...what's the right word? She's prickly."

"So I'm prickly? What's that supposed to mean?" Sienna pursed her lips for a moment as she thought about his comment. If he meant she was strong, she could live with that.

"It means you're always hiding your softness beneath a prickly shell. Sometimes I feel like if I put my hand out and touched you, I'd get scratched.

"But Aunt Caroline…hmm… I think you'd really get along with her. She's as soft as butter inside." Jack reached for his sandwich and leaned back on the sofa, munching as he watched myriad expressions cross Sienna's face. "And just like her face, yours is like an open book. When I was a kid, I stayed with her when my parents were travelling overseas, and I knew when to stay out of her way. You're the same—I can tell what you're thinking by the angle of your mouth and the depth of pink on your cheeks."

"You're making some huge jumps in your thinking there, Jack." Her foot tapped the floor again. "And not only that. You haven't got a clue what's happening here. You bowl into town. I find out you own this place and that you've changed your mind about selling it to me. Then you rock up here this morning looking like a bum surfer type, you play at being *my assistant*, you disappear for a couple of hours, and now not only do you tell me you haven't got a work ethic, but you know exactly what I'm thinking?"

"Anything else bugging you?" He lifted a brow.

"Yes, you're right. There is something else bugging me. You sure got that right. You look at me…like that… and I don't like it."

"I like looking at you." He kept his voice low, and the red in her cheeks deepened. "And I like the way you look back at me."

"Well, I've got news for you. We had our chance to get to know each other a couple of years back, but we've both moved on. You turning up here has put a big question mark over my future, and I don't like not knowing what's happening. And that's not a good basis for starting up anything."

"Anything?"

"Going out, getting together, having that date. Whatever you want to call it." Sienna turned and walked to the window across from the sofa and stared outside. "No matter that I might find you attractive, it's my exhibition and the gallery that are important to me. I'm not going to compromise my future for anyone. So stop the looking and lose any idea of getting together for that date. I have more important things on my mind."

A shot of warmth hit his chest and lingered. The spark *was* mutual, she'd as much as admitted it. Maybe they needed to do something about it?

"I *do* admire your work ethic, but don't expect the same from me. That's not why I'm here, or why I bought the place." He balled up the sandwich bag and tossed it into the crate on the floor, stood, and came across to join her at the window. "I've told you more than once already I'm not here to run the gallery or have anything to do with the day-to-day business."

She looked up at him, and her eyes were full of uncertainty. "So why are you here?"

The confident, brash Sienna had disappeared, and her hesitation planted some doubts in Jack's mind. He'd really messed up her plans. He ran his hand through his hair as he wondered whether to tell her about his own work, but he held back. It wasn't time, and he wasn't ready yet. Frustration with the situation burned in his gut.

Maybe I should just sell her the place and move on. Find another studio.

He looked around.

No. It was perfect for his work, and the truck was arriving in the morning with all his sculptures. He was itching to get to work and didn't want to wait. He'd checked out the space, and there was room in the shed to store his pieces while Sienna finished off the metal sculptures for *her* exhibition. And he had a deadline to stick to.

And he wanted to be in Noosa. Contrary to what he'd told her, he hadn't just shown up here by chance. He'd researched the place thoroughly before he'd bought the gallery two years ago, and this was where he wanted to be. As soon as he spent some time here, he intended buying a place of his own. Shame she wouldn't sell hers.

And it's where I want to work. To create the sculptures that are in my head.

He just wasn't going to let being in the gallery suck him into being involved in business. It was in his genes, and he'd fought against being like his father his whole life. He wasn't going to replicate the mess his father had made of everyone's life. He was going to focus on his art and make a successful career.

If the gallery was successful, that would be a bonus.

Jack had no commitment to anything or anyone, apart from the completion date for his sculptures. He was an artist, and he'd come here to create and show his work. He had his first big commission, and that was the reason he needed to stay here and sort out what he was going to do with Sienna.

He huffed out a breath. "Okay, let's be honest here."

Her eyes were wide, and if he looked closely, he suspected there was a glimmer of a tear in the corner of one.

Damn, he was a sucker for tears. He took her hands gently in his. It was time to come clean. If Sienna was going to be working for him and managing the gallery, he'd be honest with her.

"How about you stay to run the place, but we hire an assistant for you. Then after your exhibition, we'll see how it works out? I'll move out of your place and find my own apartment and the only thing you'll have to do is find a studio…or build your own?" He shot her a grin. "I'll be busy once my stuff arrives, and as much as I enjoyed playing secretary"— he straightened his shoulders and spoke confidently— "I'll be busy finishing off my pieces."

"Your what?"

"My pieces."

"What sort of pieces?" She pulled her hands away from his and stared at him.

"For my contract. I'm a sculptor. That's why I bought the gallery and the studio."

Sienna held his gaze, and her dark eyes were wide.

"That's why I said I was surprised when I read about you in the local paper. We work in the same medium. After I finish the pieces that are contracted, I'm going to start work on another series and hold my first exhibition here."

Chapter Ten

Sienna got through the afternoon—barely. Jack's bombshell about being an artist had thrown her in a spin. Luckily, there was a steady stream of tourists through the gallery, and she tried to concentrate on them. Jack's being an artist didn't bother her—not really. In a way, it added to his attraction, but the knowledge put his ownership of the gallery in a whole new light. He had contracted pieces, so he must be good. Why the hell hadn't Ana mentioned it, or did he keep his art private? Jack Montgomery? She knew the art world…but she hadn't come across his name before. Had he been hiding the truth from her deliberately? And if he had, why would he?

Who is the real Jack?

The laid-back guy she'd seen this week who wasn't fazed by anything? The wealthy playboy from Melbourne? Or an artist committed to his work? Lost in her thoughts, she tried to focus on the customers milling about the gallery. It was a busy afternoon, and she needed to concentrate on that. There was still work to be done no matter what problems she was trying to sort in her head.

A couple of times Sienna noticed Jack stroll casually through the shop, but she was busy with a customer each time. She straightened her back and continued to describe the enamelling process to an older tourist who loved the frog displays.

"What do you think?" The lady was looking up at her with an expectant smile.

"Sorry. What was that?" Sienna pushed thoughts of enigmatic Jack away.

"One of each. Shipped to Perth for me."

"One of each of this set?" They were standing in front a set of her frogs lying on different-shaped pieces of timber, carved into small logs.

The lady smiled at her. "No. I want one of each of your frog sets." Her wrinkled face lit up in a grin. "I love them all and it has been a magical visit and I want a memento of Noosa when I get home." She grabbed Sienna's arm and whispered. "You'll never guess who was having lunch where I ate."

Her excitement was infectious, and Sienna smiled back at her, delighted with the sale and the customer's enthusiasm.

"No, do tell."

"Chris Hemsworth! It has been the most amazing day."

Sienna looked around for Jack, but he was nowhere to be seen. She'd love to tell him that piece of news.

Later. In the meantime, she had about twenty-five frogs to package up and ship to Western Australia. Not a bad day's work.

***

Jack spent the afternoon visiting local stores to pick up some supplies to keep him going until the truck arrived with his stuff. It was due tomorrow, so he checked out the garage and the kiln room beneath the gallery. It was perfect for what he wanted. He'd passed through the gallery a couple of times through the afternoon and Sienna was as busy as ever, and ignored him each time he walked past her. He didn't need to read the expression on her face or see the depth of colour in her cheeks. Her back was ramrod straight, and something was bothering her.

He shook his head. Maybe telling her about his sculptures hadn't been such a good idea. She'd obviously thought he'd bought the gallery as an investment, which he had in a way. As much as he tried to convince himself and his father that he was a free spirit and his art was all that mattered, Jack knew he needed stability in his life. The contract and the thought of working in the studio here grounded him.

He'd also have to check out how much he was paying Sienna to run the place.

She was working her butt off, and as he'd walked around the village today, he'd realised that Sea View Gallery was by far the busiest gallery in the small town. Sienna had done a great job setting it up and getting it going in the short time she'd been here.

At five o'clock, he wandered back with a couple of packages in hand. Sienna was behind the glass desk looking at her iPad.

"A *very* good day." Her voice was soft, and her expression was wary.

There had been a shift in their relationship since he'd told her about being a sculptor, and he wasn't sure how to respond to her.

"We had a lot more customers in today," she said, her eyes still on the figures on the small tablet screen in front of her. "And excellent sales too. I've got a lot of work ahead. I sold quite a few of the frogs I'd planned to use for my exhibition."

"But won't that mean more work for you to replace them?

Sienna nodded absently before she lifted her head and looked at him with a frown. "Yes, it will but it was a good sale. Good for the gallery…and good for me."

Jack looked down at his clothes with a grin. Maybe he could dress up a bit if he was going to spend a bit of time in the place.

Keep it casual. "Nothing like a bum surfer look to pull the women in."

Sienna pulled a face and huffed. "I think it had more to do with Chris Hemsworth being in town today."

"Chris Hemsworth's here? And I missed him?" He laughed. "But thanks for the vote of confidence. Wait till you see *me* in my Prince Charming costume."

Her eyes widened, and he was glad to finally see her smiling. "You bought one?" She pointed to the packages he was carrying. "Really?"

"Yup. Nice tights, too." Jack grinned. "And I'm looking forward to the party."

"Me too." Sienna yawned and turned off the iPad.

"How about we go out for dinner to seal our agreement?" Jack wasn't sure how she'd take that, so he continued before she could refuse. "There are a couple more things we probably should discuss. The truck will be here in the morning with my stuff and I've had a look around. I just want to run it by you."

"It's your gallery. You can put things where you want."

"Whoa. You're in charge here. Remember?" He held his hands up. "And we compromise. I'm a nice guy."

Sienna snapped the cover of the iPad closed and stood. "I guess you are. I'm just being me. You'll get used to it."

And being her was a big act as far as he could tell. He'd like to get to know the Sienna beneath the prickly surface she showed him.

"So dinner? My treat."

"I suppose." She smiled again, and he relaxed as her face lit up.

"I'd like a shower. I've been poking about in the kilns. Let's go home first." A strange feeling filled him as the words came out and Sienna frowned. He quirked an eyebrow and smiled at her. "I mean, let's go to your place."

***

Jack rode his bike back to the cottage, and Sienna followed in her car. It had been a strange day, and she was a little unsettled. Dinner out somewhere lively might snap her out of this mood she was in. She'd get up early and do some enamelling before she opened in the morning. Throughout the day she'd moved from uncertainty, not knowing what her future was going to hold, and finally settled in a place where the worry landed deeper as the day wore on. The agreement with Jack about the gallery pleased her, even though she was going to have to find somewhere else to work, but the conversation with Georgie this morning wouldn't go away and stuck in her chest like a stone. She flicked on the radio and tried to let the music lift her. By the time she turned into the drive, the rock music had the desired effect, and she was feeling better even though she had to work out whether Jack had been lying to her, or if he just hadn't bothered to mention being an artist. He was so casual and friendly he sucked her right in. Somehow, he had the ability to get past the defences she usually had in place.

Things would work out. She would make sure they did. Planning and organisation were the key. Knowing she had to replace the pieces she'd sold today meant she had to make the best use of her time. Dinner with Jack was a luxury she probably couldn't afford time-wise, but no matter how hard she tried to resist him, his sexy grin sucked her in.

Jack was waiting for her outside the cottage, and he'd put his bike away. "Can we go back into town in your car?"

She unlocked the door and shot him a grin over her shoulder. "Bit misty for you here on the coast?" She pointed to the wet helmet in his hand.

"No, I'm used to Melbourne weather." That damned perpetual grin was still on his face.

Did nothing ruffle the man?

"I just thought it would be nice to travel in together. We could always go on the bike." His smile did something to her, and her heart gave a funny little flip as she pushed opened the door.

"This isn't a date, okay?"

"No. It's a business meeting, but we're leaving from the same place to go to the same place, so it makes sense to travel in the same car…or on the same bike?"

She put her hands on her hips. "All right. You win. It makes sense, I suppose. But it's not a date…and I don't like bikes, so we'll take my car."

"It's not a date." He repeated her words solemnly and she shot him a look. "You'll have to pick somewhere because I don't know my way around the area yet." He put his bike helmet down inside the door. "I've only got jeans or bike leathers."

"Do you like Italian?"

"I'll eat anything."

She was sure he would. "There's a nice Italian at Coolum. Great food and a live jazz band. And it's only ten minutes from the lake."

She needed some music and crowds around her to snap her out of the doldrums. Whenever she let the worry take over, the muse disappeared, and her work suffered. And she couldn't afford to have much downtime this week after that sale.

"Sounds great. Half hour?" Jack stood there looking at her, and Sienna snapped her thoughts back to present.

"You might be able to get ready in half an hour, but I'm going to have a soak in a deep bubble bath before we go anywhere." As soon as the words were out, she regretted them. The grin got wider; he was obviously using his imagination. Sienna gave him a little shove. "You go to *your* apartment and leave me in peace. I'll knock on your door when I'm ready."

"Yes, ma'am." With a final grin he disappeared down the hall, and Sienna didn't relax until she heard his door open and close.

The restaurant was crowded and noisy, and the band was playing. Jack held her chair out for her after they were shown to a discreet corner table away from the band.

"At least it's quieter here." Sienna put her bag on the floor. "We can talk. I made a list of things I want to sort out with you."

"Water?" The drinks waiter stood beside the table.

"Yes, please." Sienna pulled out her iPad. She'd taken it into the bath with her and made a list as she'd soaked in the bubbles.

Straight to business. This was *not* a date.

"We've sorted out the studio and your storage. Now we need you to make some decisions on the day-to-day running of the gallery.

"Put it away."

"What?"

"The iPad." Jack pointed to the computer on the table in front of her. "I told you, I don't want to run the gallery. Do what you want." For the first time today, he looked serious.

"But—"

"You've been doing fine. I'm happy for things to go on the way they are. Like I said earlier, we'll see what happens after your show. Then *you* decide if you want to stay, or if you want out."

Sienna frowned at him. "But—"

"If you want out at the end of the month, I'll find another manager. Now let's enjoy dinner."

"So we didn't need a *business* dinner after all?"

"No, but we will talk salary before we order. I looked into how much we've been paying you and it's not enough. The gallery has been doing so well, you need to be compensated more."

Sienna lifted her glass and sipped her water. "Well, that is very kind. I won't object." With a higher salary and selling more frogs, she would be in a better position to look around for her own place…and maybe build her studio.

"Nothing kind. Good business."

For a moment, she caught a glimpse of the businessman beneath the casual facade. He was a chameleon, that was for sure. Then his wide grin reappeared, and Jack leaned back in his chair. "Business is over now. We need dinner and you need some time out."

"What do you mean I need time out?"

Jack reached over and put his finger beneath her chin, and she pulled back a little as a tingle ran down her neck to her back. "I told you this afternoon. You have the most expressive face."

"Stop right there. Read my lips." She folded her arms to cover the thudding of her heart. "This. Is. Not. A. Date."

He held his hands out in front of him innocently. "Did I say it was?"

Sienna tilted her head to the side and studied him, and she couldn't stop the smile that was tugging at her lips. "Are you always so happy?"

He grinned at her and she rolled her eyes. He'd worn a black polo shirt with his black jeans, and if it was possible, the dark colour added to his sex appeal. She was going to have to work very hard to keep him at a distance. "Tell me about Melbourne. You said you went back to help out in the family business. That's where you know Blake from?"

Jack leaned back in his chair. "Yeah. I grew up in a wealthy family, went to the best schools, and was expected to follow the family path. My father had big plans for me. So when I dropped out of college and took off to art school, you could say he was less than impressed."

"But why the move out here?" She watched as his green eyes lit up. "You could have bought a gallery back there."

"I guess I got the idea from Blake. I met him when he worked for Dad at Home and Hardware and we clicked. A few games of golf, and he told me about his home in Queensland, and how much he loved the Sunny Coast. I came out on a trip and caught up with him. I actually bought the gallery the same week I met you at that doohickey place."

Sienna fought the rising panic that welled in her throat. She remembered how she'd been so attracted to him back then. Now his smile was sending constant shivers down her back, contrasting with the hot feeling in her chest.

"The time that Ana and Blake finally got together," she said weakly.

Fight it.

"So enough about me. Tell me about you. You and Georgie grew up here?" His green-eyed gaze locked with hers, and Sienna focused on her breathing. The shaky feeling disappeared a little as she thought of her background, and she met his gaze squarely.

"Yes. We were born in Sydney but grew up in Maleny. Our father ran off when we were little, and our mother chased after him and brought us to Queensland. Her brother and his wife took us in." Jack's eyes were fixed on hers, unblinking. She looked down. Jack's fingers were rubbing the inside of her wrist. She hadn't even been aware of him picking up her hand.

"Did you have a happy childhood after that?"

"We did. Uncle Renzo and Aunt Lucia gave us all the love we needed." She stared over his shoulder and couldn't keep the bitterness out of her voice. "Now our mother only ever comes back when she wants something."

"Parents can be a trial. I guess I was the opposite. My father smothered me, tried to put what he thought I should do over what I wanted."

She held her breath as Jack's deep voice washed over her. "That's why I'd never have children."

Well, that's one thing we agree on. "Me either."

Sienna picked up her water glass and took a long drink.

"Wine?" Jack called the waiter over. "If we have one glass you can still drive. Or if you'll trust me, I could drive that snazzy little car home."

Home?

Jack had settled in a bit too quickly for her liking. She was in *his* gallery, he was in *her* apartment, and now they were having a too-cosy dinner. And Sienna knew the riot of feelings and the trembling of her legs had more to do with his presence across the table than the hunger gnawing at her stomach. She didn't answer him, and she watched as the waiter opened the bottle. When the ruby-red liquid filled her glass, she held it up to the light, fascinated by the depth of colour. "Do you know how hard it is to replicate that ruby red?"

When he nodded, she looked at him curiously. "Tell me about your work, about your art."

Jack stared past her, and she wondered for a moment what he was thinking about. He lifted the glass to his lips and Sienna looked away. Coming out to dinner, no matter that he said it wasn't a date, had not been a good idea. She was altogether too attracted to him. Ana and Georgie were the only two people she ever let into her heart. Even Uncle Renzo and Aunt Lucia were kept at a distance; she could never quite trust. She kept her heart locked up tight, and there was no way she was going to leave herself open to be hurt. She'd fostered the prickly exterior and kept people at a distance, and she didn't like the way Jack was able to get past it. He drilled right past her defences and unsettled her. He was way too observant for her liking…and way too interested in *her.*

And I'm way too attracted to him. I'm going to have to be very careful here. She needed to brush him off a little.

His next words brought her back to the present, and she focused on what he was saying.

"I'm not sure what you'll think about it. And I have a feeling it might impact your decision to stay in the gallery."

"Why?" She tipped her head to the side. It was the most serious she'd seen him be.

"Your exhibition."

"What's it got to do with my exhibition?" Unease snaked its way to her stomach, and she picked up the wine and took a sip to cover her uncertainty. He'd seen way too much of that already over one dinner.

"Because of what I do."

"What do you mean?" It was a strange moment. Jack's expression was so intense she couldn't read him.

"In a way, our work might complement each other's."

"Jack, get to the point." Sienna lowered her voice and put her hands beneath her chin. "Will you stop beating around the bush and tell me what you're trying to say?"

"Is this the first time you've experimented with vitreous enamel? Do you have anything bigger than the frogs?" His gaze was fixed on her.

"Not in enamel," she said. "Only my paintings."

His shoulders dropped and he let out a breath as she watched.

"My enamel work is all based on small creatures. Frogs, mice, snails…sort of cutesy stuff. My first few pieces were really popular. That's why I decided to do a range of creatures," she said as he held her gaze. Jack was worrying her with his intense interest in the nature of her pieces. She had a feeling he was about to drop something she didn't like.

"That's excellent, then." He nodded.

"What are you trying to say?" Sienna tipped her head to the side waiting for his explanation.

"It *is* a coincidence, because I haven't even seen it in galleries in Melbourne recently."

She stared at him, and he hurried on. "I sculpt in copper and bronze too, and I use enamel to create pictures on my sculptures."

Sienna shook her head slowly and frowned. "So you were worried about having the same type of exhibition?" It was a coincidence. When she'd researched the process, she'd found few other artists who were using the same process. And she hadn't come across his name at all. She would have recognised it if she had. Her heart plummeted. Or maybe this was what the dinner and softening her up was all about. Maybe he'd changed his mind about her exhibition? If she was honest, she hoped he enjoyed being with her. The problem was, she found him so damned attractive, and no matter what his intentions were, all she could think about was getting close to him. Even when she was so unsure of what he wanted for the gallery, and her role in it, all she could think of was how it would feel to be held by him. If she looked into his eyes, she was a goner. She firmed her voice to push away the unwanted riot of feelings racing though her.

"Are you trying to tell me that you don't want my pieces exhibited in your gallery because it will take away the impact of yours when you have your own?" She narrowed her eyes as she thought of something else. "Wait, it's more than that. Do you think I've copied your ideas?"

Shit.

Chapter Eleven

"Of course not." Jack reached for Sienna's hand, but she pulled back.

Sienna was the most unpredictable woman he'd ever met. He'd had plenty of girlfriends, and he thought he knew his way around women pretty well. He'd learned when to say the right thing, and when to shut his mouth, and when to nod and not speak, but he was having trouble reading the mixed signals Sienna was giving out. Despite the complication of the gallery and their art, and living in the same place, he had this overwhelming need to kiss her. And he wanted her in his bed.

"Just get to the point, Jack. If you've changed your mind, spit it out." Her cheeks were flushed, and as he watched she crossed her arms in front of her chest and glared at him. "But don't lie to me."

"Settle down. There's no need to get upset."

"Well, I am. These past few days have been unnerving, and now you're about to tell me I have to find somewhere else to have my exhibition in *your* gallery, because *my* work is the same as yours?"

He shook his head. "Calm down. Where did you ever get the idea I was going to cancel your show?" He straightened in his chair. "I gave you my word that you could have it there, and I don't go back on my word."

"Well, you'd be the first man I've ever met who hasn't." Sienna's voice was sad and the look on her face dispelled the anger that had been building in his chest. "Look, this whole thing is getting complicated. Let's forget the month and the show. I'll pull out and leave your gallery all to you. You obviously have some concerns about our work being too similar?"

"No, I think it will be great for the gallery. We'll really establish a theme with the bronze and the enamelling." This time, he took her hands in both of his and held on tightly when she tried to pull back. "I've already sold my pieces, and I don't need to have an exhibition. They'll be on display in the building. You have yours organised, and I'll have my first show when I do some more work."

"No." She shook her head slowly.

"No, what? I'm not going to get angry, but you are beginning to piss me off with the little Miss Hard Done By act."

"No…I'm not being difficult. Do you really think it will work? This changes things even more."

Her cheeks flushed more deeply as he held on to her. "Nothing has changed, apart from you jumping to conclusions. All I really wanted to tell you…or all I wanted to do, was make sure you knew that I work in the same medium before the truck arrived with my stuff tomorrow and you jumped to the wrong conclusion when you saw it."

He got a glimpse of her dark eyes before she looked down.

"Your reaction tonight, when I'm trying to be honest, tells me if you'd seen my pieces unloaded tomorrow and I hadn't told you we work in the same medium, you probably would have walked."

"You're getting to know me." She shrugged. "I probably would have."

"Sienna, do you always think the worst of people?" She was hard work, but he was determined to get closer to her.

She nodded. "Until they prove themselves to me. Yes, I do."

The walk from the restaurant to Sienna's car was quiet. For the rest of the meal they'd discussed the techniques they each used, and Jack was pleased that Sienna seemed keen to see his work. She had relaxed a lot after he'd told her a bit more about his commission, and her interest was pleasing. He held the driver's door open for her before walking around to the passenger side and sliding in.

"As much as I love your car, it really is made for midgets." His knees were cramped between the seat and the dashboard. "Next time we go on a non-date, we'll take the bike. You'll love it."

And so would I. The thought of Sienna pressed up close behind him sent a pleasurable zing through his body. Jack leaned back and closed his eyes and waited for her to start the engine, but she took her time.

"Dratted car," she muttered.

Eventually there was a loud *click*, and she cursed again. Jack opened his eyes, and realised she'd been trying to start the car while he'd had his head back and his eyes closed, daydreaming about her in his arms.

He shot her a teasing glance. "Don't tell me we're going to have to walk home. We should have come on my bike."

"She's been doing this on and off for a couple of weeks. I keep meaning to get the motor looked at, but I haven't had the time. I've spent every spare minute with my frogs."

"What's wrong with it?"

"Her." Sienna shot him a cheeky glance. "It's a she, and she's old and cranky. Like I will be one day."

"Is that where I'm supposed to say you'll be a sweet old lady? And I suppose you're also hoping I know something about engines?"

"Do you?" Her lips parted as she smiled at him, and a rush of need coiled through Jack's chest. She was flirting with him.

"The very basics." He opened his door, enjoying the need that had moved and was now firmly lodged in every nerve ending in his body.

Every nerve ending.

"Open the hood and I'll see if any parts look like they're in the wrong place."

"That fills me with hope." The sarcasm was back, and he grinned. Better than the quiet tones that had touched him over dinner.

Sienna unlocked the hood using the lever inside the car, and then she followed him around to the front. He lifted the hood and held it up with one hand as he looked for the metal prop to hold it up.

"Sorry, it's broken. I'll hold it up while you look."

Luckily, they were parked beneath a streetlight, and he was able to see into the engine in front of him, but nothing stood out as being disconnected, covered with oil or water, or in the wrong place. That was about the limit of his mechanical knowledge. Sienna stood beside him quietly, stretched on her toes, holding the hood above his head. He ducked beneath her arm as he peered at the back of the engine, and the warmth of her body touched his skin. The need built higher and hotter, and he closed his eyes for a moment before he leaned forward, acting like he was still checking the engine. Standing so close without her pulling away was enticing. He muttered a few "ahs" and "hmms", so he sounded a little knowledgeable before he reached up and took the weight from her as he eased the hood down.

"Everything looks fine to me." He shrugged. "I guess we're stuck here until a mechanic shows up."

Sienna looked up at him without speaking and her dark eyes widened even further, filled with a hunger that echoed what was churning inside him. From the first time he'd laid eyes on her in that "doohickeys" shirt from the hardware store two years ago, he'd known this moment would come.

Something elemental shifted in him as his control fell away. He reached for Sienna without hesitation and turned her, lifting her to sit on the hood of the car so that her face was level with his. For a long moment, he stared into her eyes and she looked back at him, holding his gaze.

Wordless. But a thousand words passed silently between them. Jack moved, and her stifled gasp puffed gently on his lips as he cradled her small, delicate face between his hands. He brushed his thumb gently over her full bottom lip.

"I know we're not on a date, and I know you have an issue with me being your boss, but I would very much like to kiss you." Her gaze locked with his and still she didn't speak. Jack waited. He wasn't going to take what he thought she was offering until he knew for sure.

Damn the woman. He'd been reading her wrong all day and he didn't want to make the wrong call now. Sienna leaned into him and laced her fingers behind his neck. Her eyes, full of mystery and promise, remained locked on his. Her short hair, dark as the shadows of the still night around them, caught the moonlight. Her skin was warm, and the sweet fragrance of her perfume drifted across to him.

He lowered his lips and lightly touched her mouth with his. That first kiss was gentle, full of promise, and her unexpected sweetness hit him like a punch to the solar plexus. This was not the Sienna she presented to the world. Jack gathered her even closer to him, running his fingers through her silky short hair as the need to protect and comfort her sprang from some unfamiliar place deep inside him. Somehow in that kiss he felt her confusion, and her willingness to give, despite the tough exterior she showed the world.

***

Sienna shivered as a fire raced through her. Never in her life had she felt such a need, and it frightened her. She pulled back with a jerk and stared at Jack, fighting to keep her expression bland. Her response to his kiss had come without thought, and now she tried to force herself to be strong, and not lean back into him like her traitorous body was demanding.

"Well, considering we're not on a real date, that was a bit of a surprise." She tried to put a level of sophistication she wasn't feeling into her words, but it didn't come out like that. She knew her uncertainty sounded in her voice, with a hint of wariness mixed in, which was probably just as good.

"A nice one, though." Jack's face was shadowed, but she had felt his heart thudding hard against her chest as he'd held her.

Sienna slid down from the hood of the car and forced a casual smile onto her face. "It was. But now I need to do something about this car, seeing as your mechanical skills leave a bit to be desired."

This time her grin was genuine, because it had been obvious all along that he knew nothing about cars. "One more try." She opened the car door and slid into the driver's seat, relieved in one way to put some distance between them. Her heart was still thudding, and she ached to be back in Jack's arms, but she was going to listen to logic.

"Come on, start," she muttered. "Please." On the first turn of the key the engine fired. "I knew you could do it, old girl. Quick, Jack, get in before she changes her mind."

Jack climbed into the passenger seat. "Changes her mind?" He flicked a glance in her direction, and she knew he wasn't talking about the car.

"I need to get home. I have a lot of emails to send tonight. It was so busy in the gallery today, the work's piled up."

"Can't let the work wait, then." Jack settled back in the seat and she eased the car out onto the road. His tone was light, but the look he sent her was full of respect and a warm feeling filled her.

The roads were quiet, and Sienna was grateful for the monotonous swishing of the windshield wipers when a light shower of rain began to fall. She took the route along the coast that went through Peregian Beach before she turned off to the lake. The moonlight bathing the water glistened eerily through the fog. As they passed the sign for the beach, Jack turned to her and she wondered what he was going to say for a moment.

"It's a beautiful coastline. Great inspiration for the creative soul."

"It is." Sienna took a deep breath and gripped the steering wheel tightly. A connection had been forged between them tonight. Not just the kiss they'd shared, but the conversation they'd had when Jack had opened up about his sculptures. She was looking forward to seeing them.

"Thanks for tonight…and dinner." Sienna switched off the ignition after she parked in the carport next to the cottage. "I enjoyed myself."

Unsure of what Jack expected, she fumbled with the car door handle and turned to him.

"Well, I hope she starts tomorrow so I can get her to the mechanic."

"I'll have to give you a lift to the gallery if *she* won't."

Sienna's toes almost curled when Jack shot a cheeky grin in her direction. The interior of her little sports car was small, and he was way too close for comfort now that she wasn't focused on driving. She pushed the door open and grabbed her bag off the floor.

"You're determined to get me on that bike." She smiled at him as he followed her up the steps to the small porch. "But I've never been on one and I don't intend to start now."

"Where's your spirit of adventure, Sienna?" Jack was so close his breath brushed the back of her neck. She stepped away from him with a small sigh of relief when the door opened.

Thank God. She needed some time by herself to restore her equilibrium and remind herself why a fling with Jack—the boss—was out of the question.

"I put all of *my* spirit into my work."

"And I get to reap the benefits of your hard work." Jack's voice was thoughtful, and Sienna wasn't sure what he was referring to. His words had echoed her thoughts. She turned to him as he followed her to her bedroom door and looked at him from beneath her lashes. She didn't want to risk heady eye contact, not trusting the nervous little flutters running through her stomach. Sienna lowered her voice as she held the door half shut.

"What are your plans tomorrow? Are you coming into the gallery?" She lifted her chin and forced herself to look up at him, gripping the edge of the door between her fingers.

Jack held her gaze with those deep green eyes for a long moment before he smiled at her. "I'm not sure. Depends on what time the delivery truck gets here."

She'd forgotten his stuff was arriving tomorrow.

"Okay, then. I'm going in early, so I'll be at the gallery when you need to get in."

"I do have a key, remember?" His grin got wider, but his words had the effect she needed. The urge to grab his shirt and pull him into her room behind her faded as her boss spoke.

"Of course. Silly me. How could I forget? You own the gallery, don't you?" She turned away and nodded at him as she pulled the door shut. "Good night, Jack."

Chapter Twelve

Jack lay for a long time staring at the shadows on the ceiling before he went to sleep. The window was open, and the rustling of the leaves drifted in on the soft night breeze. Events of the last couple of days looped through his head like scenes from a movie, and Sienna was centre stage in every shot.

For the first time in his life, he'd really let a woman get under his skin, and the feeling bothered him. Everything she did stayed with him. He enjoyed sparring with Sienna; he loved watching the way she walked, the expressive gestures she made with her tiny hands when she was talking. And her low, husky voice was enticing.

He would love to see her sculpting—to watch those hands involved in the process of creation. There was so much at stake now that he knew how vulnerable she was. Sienna wanted the same things he did; they came from different backgrounds and were following different paths to get there. He knew the attraction was mutual. She'd said it in so many words yesterday, and the kiss they'd shared had shown him exactly how she felt. It was a shame he hadn't followed through on that date a couple of years back. There was no place for commitment or settling down in either of their lives. They could have had fun, gotten it out of their systems, and moved on. He could be the boss and she his employee without the flirting, and the skirting around the attraction between them.

And he still had to sort out the problem of them both needing the studio to work.

He had his sculptures and his deadline to worry about, and he owned the gallery. There was no way he was going to get into a relationship or tied down to a career and end up running the business himself.

Look what it did for Dad.

###

Jack woke to bright sunlight shining on his face. He yawned, swung his legs out of the bed, and wandered over to the open window. The lake was a brilliant blue, reflecting the cloudless sky above. He glanced down at his watch and grunted with surprise when he saw that it was after nine o'clock. Even after sorting out his thoughts last night, he'd still had a lot of trouble getting to sleep.

Damn. He wondered if Sienna's car had started. She should have left for the gallery by now. He sat back down on the side of the bed and listened, but there was no sound coming from the house. If she'd needed him, she would have come knocking—wouldn't she?

Jack made himself a coffee before strolling out to the back porch. Last night's light rain had washed everything clean; it was a glorious morning.

Perfect for a run.

But before he went back in for his running shoes, he couldn't help himself. He strolled down the steps and around the side of the house. There was no sign of Sienna's car.

Great. The car must have started okay and he could forget about her and focus on waiting for the truck and getting his stuff unpacked.

A quick call to the delivery company, and the driver told him he was just coming up the motorway and would meet him within the hour. He would have time for a short run before the truck arrived. He looked up at the little cottage as he stretched before his run. It was a shame Sienna wouldn't consider selling this place to him. The longer he stayed, and the more he looked around, the more he was convinced he could live here and build a studio. He could understand why she had bought it from the others; for the first time in his life he had found a place where he could combine work and home.

He'd try again. It would give her more money to buy her own gallery and studio somewhere, which seemed to be what she wanted. Maybe they could come to a deal. Money talked. He'd found that all his life.

***

"What are you doing down here?" Sienna smiled at her sister. She was surprised to see Georgie walk through the front door of the gallery. She narrowed her eyes as she took in the redness around her twin's eyes before she led her to the privacy of the studio. Luckily, the place was quiet. It was early and the tourists hadn't filled the street yet.

"Sit on the sofa. Coffee?" Sienna got Georgie settled and went back through the gallery and flicked the closed sign over before going into the small kitchen to pour them both a coffee. Georgie's voice came through the door.

"Mum came to see me last night."

"Mum? You mean Marjorie?" Sienna walked out to the studio and put the two cups on the floor next to the sofa. She'd spread her latest batch of enamelling on the coffee table and covered it with a drop sheet when she'd arrived earlier.

"Our mother." A little hiccough escaped Georgie's lips and she dug in her bag.

"Here." Sienna had a clean tissue in her pocket and thrust it at her sister. She should have guessed what brought this on. "Aunt Lucia is our mother."

Sienna took a step back, narrowly missing the coffee cups as Georgie glared at her.

"If you're not careful, you'll end up just like her." Georgie snapped out the words, her voice different.

"What?" Sienna stared at Georgie. "What the heck are you talking about?"

"You're so hard on her. She had her reasons for leaving us. She had to be hard…and in a way you're as bad as she is for not listening to her."

"How much money does she want this time?" Sienna was determined to hide how her sister's words cut her like a knife. She and Georgie rarely fought, but if her twin insisted on taking their mother's side, she wasn't going to hold back now. "I told you to tell her to call me if she contacted you again."

"She's dying." Georgie dropped her face into her hands and burst into tears. Sienna turned away, running her hands though her hair. Her chest closed and her breath hitched as she fought the tears that ached behind her eyes.

If it's true…

She stared through the window, trying to think of the right words to say, holding in her reaction. She didn't want to upset her sister anymore. The sound of the front door closing reached her, and Jack called out.

"Are you out the back, Sienna? Do you want me to keep the closed sign up?"

He peered around the door and looked into the studio.

"Morning. Your car started okay for you then? You left before I woke up. I didn't even hear you go."

Georgie leaned around Sienna with a surprised look and a sniff. "Interesting."

Jack turned to her with a broad smile. "Hello, Georgie, I didn't see you there."

"It's not what it sounds like." Sienna managed to compose herself before turning to Jack. "Look, we're having a private conversation here. Can you leave us alone?" She softened her tone and gave him a small smile. It wasn't his fault. "Please?"

"No problem. The delivery truck followed me into town, so I'll head out the back. Where would I find the key to the back garage?"

"It's on the hook beside the kitchen light switch, the one with the red tag." Sienna put her hands on her hips and waited for him to leave, but he stood there—all six feet of him, pure male testosterone, in running shorts and a tank top. Sex appeal oozing out of every pore.

"Everything okay here?"

Sienna's mouth dried. Jack lifted his hand and ran it though his damp hair. The muscles rippled beneath his tight shirt.

"Fine." She knew her voice was husky, and she waited for him to leave. Hell, she could barely catch her breath.

He smiled at her and disappeared through the door.

"That was quick." Georgie wiped her eyes and looked at Sienna. "What's going on?"

"Nothing." Sienna walked over to the sofa and slumped beside her twin. "Don't jump to conclusions. He's staying in the apartment at the back of the cottage while I use the studio. Just for a couple of weeks." She looked up at the shelves with a frown and muttered half under her breath. "If I ever get time to work."

"It would be a bit distracting having him around to look at all day." Georgie wiped her eyes and a smile crossed her face.

"That's not what I meant. I'm just...busy. And I've got a lot on my mind." Sienna sat straight and tucked her leg beneath her. "Now tell me what else *she* said that you had to drive all the way down here to tell me."

"I had to come down here anyway. And it's not the sort of thing I wanted to talk about on the phone." Georgie patted the bag beside her. "Blake was supposed to come down to

Noosa to get some papers signed, but I offered to come so I could see you on the way." She dabbed at her eyes again with the tissues. "Now I have to clean myself up a bit before I meet this guy. He's the solicitor for some famous author that the store is doing a renovation for."

Sienna folded her arms. "I know you think I'm hard, but Marjorie knows you're a soft touch. Did she ask you for money?"

"Well—"

The sound of a truck beeping as it backed up the back driveway interrupted Georgie's words.

Sienna rolled her eyes. "Whatever happened to my peaceful life?" She pushed herself to her feet and crossed to the kitchen door before pushing it open. "Jack, your truck's here."

He wandered through casually, cup of coffee in hand, and headed out to meet the truck driver.

"He's going to drive me crazy. I guess that's what being wealthy does for you. Nothing ever seems to bother him. He is so laidback." Sienna shook her head and held her hand out to Georgie. "Come on. Let's get out of here and grab a real coffee, and we'll figure out what to do."

Sienna moved to the door and tried to push away that feeling that her life was about to change.

###

By the time Sienna got back to the gallery and flicked the sign on the door to open, there was no sign of Jack or the truck, and she heaved a sigh of relief. She had enough to think about—a gallery to run, her frogs to get finished in two weeks, and an exhibition to organise, and dealing with the riot of feelings Jack set afire in her. And the only way she'd managed to calm Georgie was to promise to see Marjorie when she was in Montville for Faith's birthday party, the weekend after next. Apparently, their dear mother had moved back to the area and needed money for medical treatment.

Or so she said.

What if their mother really was ill?

Sienna rubbed a weary hand over her eyes. This time last week she'd been full of excitement about buying the gallery and her upcoming exhibition. She got through the afternoon, sold a few big pieces, interviewed two artists who were looking for a venue for a show, and took a dozen phone calls. She couldn't wait until Katy, a young artist, started work as her assistant. That had been one of the positive changes in the past week.

Jack had lightened the load by getting the mail and bringing her coffee. If only she could forget about how good he looked.

There had been no sign of him since this morning, which should have suited her just fine. But she hadn't stopped looking up eagerly every time the door opened. At five o'clock, she closed the gallery and headed downstairs to turn the kilns on. She was going to spend a few hours on her pieces. She'd promised Georgie she'd stay overnight after Faith's party, so that would be another day out of her preparation time. As she walked down the steps she flicked a curious glance toward the garage. There was a shiny new padlock on the door. It would be interesting to see Jack's work. She had been curious about his methods since he'd described them at dinner the other night. As soon as he came back from wherever he'd gone, she'd ask him to show her, but in the meantime, she had work to do.

###

Five hours later with her hands on her hips, Sienna studied the array of pieces on the studio shelves. A row of frogs in a variety of positions in bright hues of green, red, and blue looked back at her. She yawned and debated whether to go down and enamel the last of tonight's batch, but before she could decide, the sound of a motorcycle pulling up at the back of the building caught her attention.

Her heartbeat picked up and she smoothed her hair down. She'd been perspiring in the heat of the small bricked-in room, and her hair was plastered to her head. Heading for the bathroom to clean up, she pulled off her thick work apron and then stopped before she got to the door.

What the heck am I doing?

She turned and crossed the room to the door to the back of the building. Jack was walking across to her, with his helmet in his hand.

"Are you okay?" He put his helmet on the ground, held the top of her arms and frowned down at her. "When it got so late, I was worried about you."

A strange warm flush filled Sienna's chest as he held her gaze, his brow wrinkled in a frown. It had been a long time since anyone had worried about her. Her stomach fluttered and she fidgeted beneath his touch.

"I'm fine. I've been working on my frogs." She stepped back and rubbed her arms with her hands, trying to ignore the sensation of his hands on her skin. She glanced over at the sofa. "I was thinking about sleeping here tonight."

"I was worried your car wouldn't start."

"Oh, damn." Sienna rolled her eyes. "I totally forgot about the car. I didn't call the mechanic."

"Have you eaten?"

"What are you, my keeper?" Sienna was sorry as soon as the words left her lips.

"I didn't mean to upset you. I was just trying to look out for you." He shrugged. "Besides, I had to come back in. There's some stuff here in the garage I need."

She'd forgotten all about the truck delivery this morning, and her curiosity was piqued. "Did everything arrive okay?"

"Yes. I just need to get myself organised now."

"Jack? Will you show me your work?" Her voice was hesitant. Maybe he didn't want her to see his work yet. Uncertainty filled her as he stared down at her.

He hesitated and she shrugged. "If you don't want to—"

"No." He walked over to the small loading area next to the door and put his helmet down. "It's fine. Employee confidentiality and all that. I'm sure you won't share what I show you with anyone."

Disappointment settled in Sienna's chest. He was worried she'd take his ideas, and he'd found it necessary to remind her she was an employee. For a while tonight as she'd immersed herself in her work, she'd totally let the situation leave her thoughts.

"On second thought, don't worry about it." Sienna turned away and strode across to the door, her protective work boots making a satisfying clump as she walked. "I'm going back down to the kiln. I'll lock up when I leave here." She was almost to the door when warm fingers descended on her shoulder. She turned and looked up at Jack, knowing she was being snarky, but the unwanted feelings bubbled to the surface as the smell of his cologne surrounded her. "Thanks for checking on me anyway."

His fingers held her lightly and her shoulder almost sizzled from the warmth of his touch. She shrugged his fingers off. "What now?"

"I was going to wait for you to finish in case your car won't start." He held her gaze. "Would you mind if I came down and watched you work? When you're finished, I'll show you my pieces if you still want to see them."

Sienna stepped back and leaned against the doorframe. Her heartbeat was picking up, and her hands were trembling a little. A strange light feeling in her arms and legs matched the fluttery feeling in her chest. The hard wood of the doorframe pressed against her back and she focused on that as she slipped her hands into the pocket of the protective apron.

She hadn't eaten. She needed to eat. *That's why I'm all shaky. It's nothing else.*

Something shifted, just a little, and her resistance crumbed as all sensible thought took flight. She was tired of fighting it. Before she could stop herself, her hands came out from her pockets and she took a step toward him. Stepping up on her toes, she reached up, slid her hands up the front of his shirt, and held his face with both hands. His skin was warm beneath her fingers and the bristles of his unshaven chin rasped against her fingers.

"If we don't get this out of the way, I'm not going to be able to focus on my work," she whispered. She held his gaze and watched Jack's lips head toward hers. She closed her eyes in anticipation, and the soft puff of his breath warmed her lips.

Then nothing. Apart from the touch of his forehead resting on hers.

She opened her eyes and pulled back away from him a little.

"I thought you wanted to keep us on a business level." His voice was soft, but the husky note betrayed the way he was feeling.

Or she hoped it did. It wasn't fair if she was the only one fighting this.

"You said no dates, so I thought that would mean no messing around, too."

Laughter bubbled up through her chest, and Sienna didn't fight it as the giggle spilled over. "Messing around?"

"Well, isn't that what we were about to do?"

Sienna stepped back, relieved Jack had broken the tension building between them. "I guess it was. But you're right. We'll stick to what we agreed on."

She turned on her heel and pushed the door open and looked over her shoulder at him. "Come on, of course you can watch me work."

Chapter Thirteen

A blast of warm air hit them as Sienna pushed the door open. Jack was surprised at the size of the room beneath the gallery, and his interest was piqued immediately. With a kiln room this large at his disposal, he could work around the clock if necessary to meet his deadline.

Once they sorted out who was going to work where.

Three small kilns were placed along the back wall, and two large tables ran along the centre. Sculpting wax and containers of ground enamel filled a set of shelves beside the door. The tables were covered with a variety of small linear animal figures in various stages of the process. For a moment he forgot that Sienna was there as he wandered over to the table and picked up one of the small bronze figures. He held it up to the light and smiled as the colours merged into one another and deepened when he moved it around in his fingers.

"So?"

He glanced across at Sienna, and his smile grew. She was standing, hands on hips and a frown on her face.

"So what?"

"Do you think I'm kidding myself, or are they worthy of an exhibition?"

Jack held the small sculpture up to the light. It was a butterfly in the midst of flight, and its wings were enamelled in a variety of blues from the palest eggshell in the middle, to a deep cobalt on the wingtips. He twirled it around. It was small and delicate, very different from his work.

"It's beautiful. You're very talented. But I already knew that from the frogs in the gallery." He put it carefully back on the table and lifted his gaze to meet hers. "And I'm interested to hear about the process you use. The depth of colour you've achieved has escaped me so far with my glazing, but my sculptures are life-size and it's harder to get an even depth of colour over the metal."

Jack watched Sienna visibly relax beneath his gaze. She dropped her hands to her sides and rolled her shoulders. A small smile played about her lips, and the colour in her cheeks deepened as a soft rosy tinge stained her skin. "Hmph…well, thanks." If he didn't know better, a slight lack of confidence was coming out from beneath her usual sassy exterior.

She walked to one of the kilns and turned the temperature gauge up. "Pull up a stool and you can watch me for a while." She shot him a grin, and a jolt hit him in the solar plexus as her full lips curved upward. "Watch and learn."

My pleasure, thought Jack as he held her gaze. She was the first to look away as she turned to the kilns along the back wall.

Not sure about the learning, but the watching will be mighty enjoyable.

He slid onto the stool and leaned back against the counter when Sienna lifted the door of the kiln open with one fluid movement. She untied her apron and put it on the table before taking her long-sleeved shirt off and slipping the apron back on. Jack's breath caught in his throat when she turned to the shelves next to the door and stretched high on her tiptoes to reach for a container of ground enamel. She wore a pair of shiny black leggings, which he was beginning to recognise as her signature work pants. The pants hugged her like a second skin, and the bright red sleeveless cropped T-shirt clung to her back. The heat protective apron covered her from shoulder to knee in the front, and only the ties crossed behind her.

    She turned and glanced across at him as she placed the enamel on the table and slid across a crate filled with pieces of copper and bronze. His gaze lingered on her long, narrow fingers, watching her lift the pieces carefully and place them in a row along the edge of the table. After she removed the coloured metal shapes waiting to be coloured, she lifted the crate back onto the shelves, and Jack dropped his gaze to the well-defined muscles flexing at the top of her arms. Her small biceps were sculpted, and her strength surprised him. Dozens of small frog figurines were soon laid out on the worktable.

    Sienna might be petite, but she was strong, and he was beginning to realise how physically hard she worked running the gallery all day and then coming down to this hot cavern to work at night. His respect for her increased, and he wrinkled his brow in a frown. Hopefully the new assistant would lighten her workload. But she was busy now; they'd talk about her handing over more of the work later. In the meantime, he was going to enjoy watching her work. The temperature in the room increased as the kilns heated up to their baking temperature. Jack brushed away a trickle of perspiration from the back of his neck.

"When I add the water to the enamel powder, I pretend I'm making pancake batter." The tip of her tongue poked through her lips as she focused on stirring the liquid. Her brow wrinkled with concentration when she tipped the water into the enamel powder.

"Sometimes I get impatient." She shot him a look and laughed. "I know, that's me. I like to work fast, but this process has taught me to slow down. I used to think, 'I'll just add a bit more liquid this round,' and I'd inevitably end up with it too runny and it wouldn't stick. I lost one whole batch a couple of weeks ago. It's a wonder you didn't hear me ranting all the way down in Melbourne."

"So what did you find was the best way?" Jack was still experimenting with the coatings on his sculptures.

"Well, it depends on the metal, but it's a bit like cooking pancakes. It's good to rest the enamel before you start using it, and of course it settles between uses, so always stir it if it's been sitting for a while."

"I've never cooked pancakes."

She lifted her head and tipped it to the side as her dark gaze locked on him. "Never?"

"I don't cook much at all." Jack ran his hand through his hair, surprised to find it already damp from perspiration as the room heated up.

Sienna had a slight tinge of pink on her cheeks, but still looked fresh.

"Hmm. I forgot for a while you were the spoiled rich boy."

"That's a bit harsh." A rare fragment of temper tugged at him. She really knew how to push his buttons, and he fought it down. "I ate out most of the time because that's the way everyone lives in Melbourne."

"I thought you lived on your parents' estate. That's what Ana told me."

"I had an apartment near the city, but I moved back home after Dad had his heart attack."

"And I suppose you had servants to cook your pancakes?"

Jack stared at her. "Servants? We had people who were employed to help out." His eyes narrowed as a small giggle escaped her lips, and he realised she'd been teasing him all along and he'd fallen for it.

"Well, remind me to teach you how to make pancake batter, and then you'll have no trouble with the enamelling mix."

Her lips were full, and she had the prettiest mouth. Whenever she was brushing a difficult edge, the tip of her tongue appeared as she leaned closer to the frog in her hand and focused her attention on the gentle movement of the enamelling brush. Her black eyeliner was smudged from where she'd rubbed her eyes, and Jack couldn't be sure if the smudge of shadow on the delicate skin under her eyes was from the kohl she wore, or because she was tired. All he knew was that whenever she moved, he couldn't keep his eyes from her. He was aware of every inch of her. His gaze travelled from the short pixie haircut, down her long graceful neck, to her petite body. The snug-fitting T-shirt beneath the work apron outlined her small breasts. He deserved a medal for reminding her about their business relationship when she'd grabbed his shirt before. Looking down at her lips and not kissing her had been tough, but he didn't want to ruin things between them.

Sienna finished the piece she was working on, and with a soft grunt of satisfaction she held it up to the light, before turning to put it on the shelf farthest from the heat. Jack swallowed when she stood on her tiptoes to put it with the other finished pieces. The form-fitting pants and T-shirt hugged her curves, and his mouth was suddenly dry.

Damn shame they had this business agreement, because all he could think about was the feel of her leaning against him and her lips against his. Jack pushed the stool back and cleared his throat. It was time to get out of here before he did something he'd regret. They'd made a deal, and he'd keep his end of it.

"Are you finished now?" He glanced down at his watch. "It's almost midnight. You're not going to get much sleep."

"I'm going to sleep upstairs." She stood back and gestured to the door. "You go and do whatever you came here for, and I'll lock up down here." She rubbed her arms with those long slender fingers, and he fought the longing to have them running up his chest again.

"Fine. I just need to get a couple of things to take back to your place." He didn't move and kept his gaze on her. "Then I'll show you my pieces if you still want to see them."

"I do." She shrugged those delicate shoulders. "Are you going back upstairs?"

"Yes." He moved to the door and turned back to her. "But I won't go back to your place till you're in the studio."

"Thank you. That's nice of you, but there's no need to hang around. It's safe here."

"I'll wait for you upstairs." He let himself out without looking back at her and headed for the locked room to collect his gear.

***

When the door closed behind him, Sienna let her breath out with a whoosh and sat on the stool Jack had vacated. It sure was a change to have someone looking out for her, and it felt good. No matter how laid-back he was, and how much that annoyed her, Jack was a gentleman.

She'd been fully aware of his gaze fixed on her while she worked, and she'd enjoyed answering his questions. Teasing him was fun too, despite the warm shivers that skittered down her back every time he asked her something in that deep and sexy voice. She'd worked alone with her sculpting and enamelling for two years now. Georgie and Ana were skilled in carpentry, but they had no knowledge of the artistic processes she'd experimented with since she'd moved to the coast. Jack's interest had been gratifying. Knowing the process, he appreciated how hard it was to get it right.

So maybe she'd stretched a little higher and for longer than she would have if he hadn't been there. Her thoughts scattered, she moved across to the kilns and switched them off. He'd reminded her their relationship was about business. And that's the way it would stay, no matter what her traitorous body was trying to tell her. Listen to logic; her future depended on it.

"Shit." A sharp edge of one of the unfinished pieces pierced the palm of her hand when she picked up the last tray. She dropped it onto the shelf and held her fingers up. Blood was trickling down the side of her hand, and she moved across to the sink and rinsed it off. The cut wasn't deep, but it was long, and blood seeped out even after she washed it. She curled her fingers to put pressure on the cut, and the blood stopped dripping. The first aid kit was upstairs in the kitchen. Sienna untied her apron with one hand and shrugged it off before uncurling her fingers.

Damn, the cut was still bleeding. *That's what happens when I daydream.*

She dabbed at the cut with her apron before wrapping it around her bleeding palm. Flicking the light off with her good hand, Sienna pulled the door of the kiln room shut, grateful for the light that spilled down out of the storage shed. It had rained while they were inside, and the wet cobblestones glistened in the moonlight. Ragged dark clouds scudded across the sky and the wind pushing them along brought a tang of salt air from the beach. She'd been so busy she hadn't been for a walk on the beach in days. Soon, she promised herself. It would help clear the cobwebs that seemed to be ensnaring the common sense that usually guided everything she did.

Getting tangled up with Jack was the least logical path she could take. She really had to brush him off. But she didn't want to…

Jack was banging around in the storage shed, and Sienna poked her head around the door. She looked around the boxes filling the small space, and her breath caught. She raised her hand to her mouth. "Oh, my goodness."

Two huge abstract sculptures stood on either side of the piled-up moving cartons. She walked over and ran her fingers down the fluid shape of the one closest to the door. "These are yours?"

Jack's face was shadowed, and she looked up at him, unable to read his expression.

"Yeah. The rest are still in the basement at my parents' place." His voice was tight, and she wondered if he was shy about his work.

She lifted her chin, caught his gaze, and challenged him to hustle her from the room. "They're amazing. They make my pieces seem trivial." Then all of a sudden, her confidence disappeared as unexpected doubt rushed in. His pieces were spectacular. His artistic flair showed in every curve and angle of the pieces. For a moment it made her feel as though her pieces were insignificant.

Am I kidding myself thinking I'm good enough to show my work in an exhibition? In Noosa of all places?

Sienna stepped back and put one hand behind her, feeling for the door handle. "Wait." Her eyes met his, and all thoughts of sculptures, frogs, and shows fled and she caught her lip between her teeth as Jack followed her to the door. She could read the expression in his green eyes as clear as day. It mirrored the feelings racing through her.

He stood beside her and took her shoulders gently between his hands. Sensual intent filled his gaze, and a shiver started low in her stomach and travelled in every direction. She couldn't look away. She couldn't resist the feelings rampaging through her as he held her; accepting them came to her as naturally as breathing.

"What's wrong with your hand?" He looked down at her hand, which had the apron fisted against her chest.

"Just a little cut."

"Show me."

He pulled her closer and unwound the apron from around her hand. "Damn. That's a nasty gash there. What did you do?"

"I caught it on one of the rough edges when I was packing up." At least talking about her hand dispelled the mood that had ensnared them briefly. "It's nothing. I'll just go clean it and put a bandage on it." She pulled away from him. "I'll see you in the morning."

"Not so fast." A warm hand held her shoulder gently. "I'll do it for you. Working one-handed is a bit hard."

"It's all right, Jack. I said I'll do it." Sienna knew her voice was testy, but being with him in the confined space, sharing her work with him, and then seeing his, had created an intimacy between them she didn't want. Okay, maybe she did want it, but it would complicate things way too much.

She moved away from him and wasn't surprised when he followed her into the studio.

"Where's your first aid kit?"

"In the cupboard under the sink in the kitchen."

Jack took her arm and pulled her over to the sofa before gently pushing her to sit down. "Sit there and don't move." He stared at her for a moment. "And there's no need to be sassy."

Sienna leaned against the soft back of the sofa, closed her eyes, and rested her head on the cushion. Her hand had started to throb, and her neck ached from working. As soon as Jack finished his first aid ministrations, she was going to sleep. It looked like there was no way she was going to get rid of him until she allowed him to look after her.

Which was kind of nice in a way.

"How often do you work here alone?"

She opened her eyes. She must have dozed off. He was crouched down in front of her and had placed a bowl of water on the floor.

"Most nights. Why?"

"It's not safe."

"I'm a big girl now, Jack."

"What if you'd cut yourself badly and passed out or something?" He unwound the apron from around her palm, and she drew a quick breath as the dried blood stuck to the fabric. "You could burn yourself...or start a fire."

"But I didn't."

"It's my gallery and my building, and I need to make sure that my staff are safe." His voice was firm.

A slow burn began in her stomach when Jack dipped a cotton pad in the water and cleaned her hand.

My staff.

She'd been kidding herself about this intimacy between them. His comment brought her back to earth. It served as a good reminder of what their relationship really was. She bit back the words that were boiling inside, took a deep breath, and let the anger recede. He was her boss, and he owned the gallery. There was nothing she could do about it, and there was nothing to be gained by getting angry. She'd been there and done that already. She'd agreed to give it a month. Once her show was done, she would decide what to do next. Sienna bit her lip and frowned. The more she thought about it, the more she realised that working alongside Jack was problematic. But no matter what logic she used to convince herself she could get over this attraction to him, her body wouldn't cooperate.

"Any deeper and you would need stitches."

Sienna kept her eyes closed and her head back against the sofa. The sharp aroma of antiseptic liquid reached her before the warm pressure of a Band-Aid filled her palm.

"There you go. I don't think it needs more than that."

She opened her eyes when he let her hand go, and she gestured to the first aid stuff on the floor. "Leave all that. I'll clean it up in the morning."

"No. I'll do it. Do you want a glass of water or a coffee or something?" Jack gathered up the bowl and the ointment, and the box of bandages, and held his hand out for the apron that was still on her lap.

"For someone who's used to servants, you're pretty versatile." She shot him a grin. "Thanks for looking after me."

"So have a coffee with me before I go. I need a shot of caffeine for the ride back home." He stood up in front of the sofa and his deep green gaze pinned her. Her heartbeat skittered up a notch.

"Thank you, I will." She liked having him around and was reluctant to say good-bye to him. He was easy to spend time with, and if she could put the gallery ownership aside, they had a lot in common.

Art-wise, anyway.

It was strange to sit back on the sofa and listen to Jack rattling around with the coffeemaker. Eventually, the aroma of brewing coffee drifted out from the kitchen. A pleasant sleepiness began to overtake her, and she slipped her shoes off and pulled her legs up beneath her.

"Milk and sugar?" Jack called from the kitchen.

"Yes, please. Both."

Sienna watched as he crossed the studio grasping two coffee mugs. His dark T-shirt strained against his broad shoulders as he balanced the two cups trying not to spill the hot liquid. She grinned to herself. He'd picked the biggest mugs she had in the kitchen, so he'd be here for a while yet. She slid along the sofa to the end to make room for him. He put the cups on the small table at the other end of the sofa. The sofa cushion tipped when he sat next to her, and she grasped the cushion with her uninjured hand, so she didn't slide down on top of him.

"Thanks for letting me watch you work. I really enjoyed spending time with you tonight." Jack turned and slid his arm along the top of the sofa. His words mirrored her thoughts.

Uh-oh.

"I usually prefer to work alone." She crossed her arms in front of her chest and tried to keep her voice snappy. Having six feet plus of attractive male sitting so close to her when she was tired and feeling vulnerable was not her choice for sensible behaviour.

"Why are you so defensive, Sienna?" Jack held her gaze and his voice was low. "Who hurt you?"

"No one hurt me. I just prefer to be alone." She didn't like the little bit of need she could hear in her own voice, and she lifted her chin. "That's the way I am."

"Why? We all need people in our life, and around us. I've seen you with Ana and Georgie. That's not being alone."

"That's different. Georgie is my sister, and we've been friends with Ana all our lives." She stared at him. "And who's going to be around you once you get settled here, anyhow? It's a bit like the pot calling the kettle black. Unless you've got a heap of artist friends out here?"

She knew she was babbling, but his intense gaze fixed on her unnerved her. Sienna leaned forward to reach for her coffee mug, but Jack grabbed her hand. She held his gaze, and something elemental moved inside her when he put his arms around her. She tried to pull back from his hold, but he tightened it.

"Sienna?" His green eyes held a question as she looked up at him. He lifted his hand and brushed his thumb over her lip.

Her breath caught in her throat as a riot of unfamiliar feelings spiralled through her.

"Oh, what the hell." She pulled her hand away from his, rose to her knees, and grabbed his face with both hands. "I'll probably regret this in the morning, but we're going to have to get this out of the way."

Sienna leaned forward and pressed her lips against his…and it was heaven. He lifted his arms and slid her across to his lap without breaking the contact. She fit into the curve of his shoulder so naturally…a perfect fit.

"Are you sure?" His words vibrated against her lips as his arms tightened around her. She couldn't move away even if she changed her mind. She slid her hands down past his shoulders and gripped the tops of his arms, smiling as his muscles tightened beneath her fingers. Sienna lifted her head just long enough to answer, and Jack's lips moved across her cheek and down her neck.

"We need to do something about this attraction…and then we can move on," she said.

The feel of his hard chest against her, the slide of his lips down her throat, slammed into her, and the heat rushed in. Sienna closed her eyes and sank into the pleasure he was offering.

Chapter Fourteen

Sienna slipped Jack's T-shirt over her head and walked across the studio toward the sofa. Jack grinned up at her and held out his hand, but she ignored him.

"Where are the clothes you had on last night?" He shot her a lazy grin.

"You tell me and we'll both know."

"They must be here somewhere. Come back and we'll look together." He raised himself up on one elbow, but she shook her head and pursed her lips at him.

"As tempting as that may be, it's almost time to open the gallery. I've got an appointment with the newspaper at eleven a.m." She pointed to the clock above the door; it was almost ten thirty.

"So, mister, you need to get dressed and look like a gallery owner."

"Have we got time for breakfast? Pancakes, maybe?" The look on his face was comical and she shook her head.

"Someone has to run this gallery, so once I'm showered and dressed you can have the bathroom."

"And then we can go out for a quick breakfast?" He tried to put on a pleading expression, but it didn't work.

"When you decide to get up, can you make up the bed please?"

"Guess I'm not going to get lucky then?"

Sienna stood in the doorway away from the temptation of his reach. "Last night was fun, Jack. We've dealt with what was building between us, now we move on. Okay?"

The whole night had been…fun.

"Fun" was probably the best word to use. Two consenting adults giving in to a mutual attraction and doing something about it. They'd laughed and giggled and enjoyed each other's company. And given each other a great deal of pleasure…the soft teasing, the laughter and their banter had enhanced her night… and their lovemaking. Sienna hummed softly as she stripped down and stepped into the shower.

They'd move on, their relationship would go back to business; she'd have her exhibition, then decide if she was going to stay at the Sea

View Gallery. All logical, and cut-and-dried, and she had a month to sort it out. So why did she feel so excited, and why was that silly grin plastered on her face?

###

Sienna managed to put Jack to the back of her mind when the reporter from the local paper arrived, and she approved the ads they were going to run for her show. After that, she focused on her email and the satisfying number of inquiries that were starting to arrive. The word about Sea View Gallery was getting out, and hopefully her debut show would cement that.

The morning flew by, but there was no sign of Jack in the gallery. He was either having a very long breakfast or he'd gone back out to Forest Lake. No matter how many times Sienna glanced at the door at the back of the gallery, he didn't make an appearance, and she pushed away the little tug of disappointment that insisted on staying with her. Maybe he'd gone back home; maybe he was unpacking some of his boxes in storage. Anyway, it was none of her business, and she wasn't going to go out to find him.

Move on. I've got a heap to do or my exhibition will never get off the ground.

Just after noon, when the gallery had cleared for the usual slow time during lunch, the front doorbell tinkled softly. Sienna looked up from the iPad where she was checking her afternoon appointments. A tall, elegantly dressed woman about her age stood in the doorway looking around the gallery as if for someone in particular. A designer-label dress, Sienna thought, if she knew her fashion, and the shoes were definitely Jimmy Choos. She'd salivated over the very same pair in a trendy shoe shop in Brisbane the last time she'd gone there on a shopping expedition with Georgie and Ana. She loved clothes and indulging her sense of fashion, but in her work, heels were impractical. She stared at the woman's feet—oh, she loved those shoes.

The woman turned to Sienna with a frown, but from her height she still managed to look her up and down. Sienna stood and straightened and plastered a smile on her face. All kinds came into the gallery, and they were all prospective customers.

"Hello. Welcome to Sea View Gallery." Sienna picked up an information brochure and held it out, but the woman ignored it, so she dropped it back on the table with a shrug. "If there's anything I can help you with, please ask." She gestured to the gallery and then turned back to her iPad.

"I'm here to see Jack Montgomery." The woman's voice was as impatient as her expression, and a frown marred her perfectly made-up face. Sienna got the impression that she'd done something to upset this visitor but didn't have a clue what it could be because she'd never seen this woman before.

"Do you have an appointment?" Sienna pretended to refer to the iPad. Jack had made it quite clear she was running the gallery and he would stay in the background, so maybe it was personal? "Who shall I say is calling?" Sienna smiled, trying to keep the interaction pleasant despite the woman's snooty behaviour.

"Arielle."

"And your last name…"

"Jack knows who I am." A perfectly manicured hand reached up and smoothed the blonde hair, which was sprayed into place.

"If you say so, but I'm not even sure if he's in." Sienna was reluctant to go out the back and look for him, and this woman was pushing her buttons. "I'll take a message and make an appointment for you, Ms....?"

The woman stared at her and shook her head slowly. She put her bag on the floor and sauntered over to the love seat beside the glass desk. She draped herself over the seat and smiled at Sienna before trilling a little girlish laugh.

"There's no need for that. I'll wait here. I'm Jack's partner."

Chapter Fifteen

Jack revved the bike and hit the coast road. He'd needed some fresh air and some time to clear his head. Last night with Sienna had been magic, but then she'd put the walls back up this morning. Maybe she'd been focusing on having to open the gallery. Or that's what he was hoping. He wasn't used to being put in his place and told where a relationship could go. Last night had given him a lot to think about. Maybe seeing each other wouldn't complicate things too much; they were both adults and the night had been fun. They could separate business and pleasure. Surely, she could see that, too?

  The relaxed Sienna was even more beautiful, and he hadn't been able to keep his eyes—or his hands—off her. There should be more of it. Life was for loving, and it was easy for him to become impatient with people who took things too seriously. His father was a prime example of that.

She'd declined to join him for breakfast, so now he'd take Sienna out for lunch and use his best persuasive techniques to convince her they could do business and…sex.

And be friends as well.

And it wouldn't impact anything. They were adults and could handle it as long as they were honest with each other. Jack had seen too much dishonesty back in Melbourne, both in business and in his personal life, and it had been one of the reasons for coming out west and starting afresh.

Honesty. That was the key.

The sweet salt-laden air rushed past and Jack took a deep breath as he turned the bike back toward Noosa. No matter what his reason had been, this move was the best damned thing he'd ever done in his life.

Five minutes later, Jack put his helmet on the sofa in the studio and smoothed his hand over his hair. He was quickly getting the impression that when he was in the gallery, he was supposed to look the part of the owner and not like a surfer bum. He pushed the door open and glanced around. The gallery was almost clear.

So, lunch it is.

Sienna was standing at the glass desk by the door. He walked up behind her quietly and put his arms around her waist and nuzzled her neck.

"Let's go have lunch. I missed out on breakfast."

"Jack Montgomery!"

His head flew up at the familiar voice, and Sienna stiffened beneath his hands as the shrill voice hit him.

Oh, damn. He thought he'd left all that behind him. "Arielle? What are you doing here?"

She lifted herself gracefully from the love seat where she'd been reclining, drew herself to her full height, and strode over to the table. She was almost six feet tall and towered over Sienna, who moved away behind the counter, a closed expression on her face.

"More to the point, what's going on here?" Arielle pointed to Sienna before she stepped up to him and put her arms around his neck. "But no matter, I'm here now. You can take me out to lunch." She pouted her little signature pout. "I've missed you, baby."

A snort came from behind the counter and Jack glanced over at Sienna at the same time as he disentangled Arielle's arms from around his neck. Arielle still wore the same cloying perfume that had always given him a headache, and he rubbed his hand across his eyes. Her timing couldn't have been any worse. By her stiff posture, he could sense Sienna withdrawing from him more by the second, and he needed to get Arielle out of here.

"What are you doing here?" He moved away from her and glanced at Sienna. She was looking at her iPad and focused on the screen. He'd sort this out right now and make it clear that Arielle was an unexpected visitor—and from his past.

"I came to see you. I thought it was time we sorted out that silly little matter you raised when you left."

"You flew all the way from Melbourne just to talk to me? Why on earth would you do that?"

Now Sienna was looking from one to the other, a small smile playing at her lips. The doorbell above the entry tinkled and she waved dismissively at Jack before she turned to greet the customer. "You pair of *lovebirds*"—despite the smile, her voice was sarcastic— "go out and have lunch. I'll look after the gallery."

"What? Wait a minute—" But Jack was interrupted by a customer who walked timidly to the counter. He turned to Sienna and watched the colour drain from her face as she saw the small, red-haired woman standing behind Arielle. Her face was thin and drawn, and she clutched her bag to her chest as though someone was about to take it from her.

"Now my day has gone to absolute and total crap," Sienna muttered.

The woman stepped forward and held her hand out. "Sienna, I really need to talk to you."

"So I've heard, Marjorie." The sarcasm was gone and replaced by an icy tone. "We can talk, but not here."

Sienna reached out and took Jack's arm between her fingers and he glanced down, surprised by her touch but instinctively sensing she was grounding herself.

"I'm sorry. Can you look after the gallery while I take a short break?" She held his gaze, and he watched curiously as she heaved a deep breath as though trying to dig deep to keep calm.

"I'll be quick and then you can go out with your *partner.*" Sienna flicked a gaze at Arielle, who had followed the whole exchange with interest.

Jack put his hand on top of Sienna's fingers to keep her hand there.

Who was this woman who had Sienna so rattled? A warm protective feeling suffused his chest and he wanted to put his arms around her and hold her close. Waves of distress were coming off her, and he knew this woman was more than a customer with a problem.

He lowered his head and spoke softly. "Are you okay?"

Sienna waved her hand dismissively as she stepped away from him. "I just need to have an hour, and I'll be back. Then you and *Arielle* can go have lunch."

"Of course, I can mind the gallery. Take as long as you like."

"I won't need long." She stared at the older woman and a shiver ran down Jack's back as she spoke.

"I'll meet you in the coffee shop next to the post office in fifteen minutes. Then I'll give you ten minutes, so make it good." Sienna disappeared through the door at the back of the gallery before he could speak. Arielle took his arm as the small woman left by the front door.

"Who are they, Jack?" The little-girl voice she put on was grating on him already.

***

Sienna went straight to the bathroom and splashed her face with cold water. She gripped the edges of the cold basin, her hands shaking. She took a deep breath, trying to gain a measure of calm before she left the gallery to meet Marjorie. She had stopped thinking of her as Mum years ago.

What a morning. Double whammy. First Jack's girlfriend appears and then Marjorie waltzes into Sea View Gallery. It was the first time she'd seen her in three years, and she'd aged considerably. And if she could be believed for once, she did look quite ill. She'd lost a lot of weight, and her skin had a yellowish tinge.

Picking up the towel, Sienna patted her face dry and applied another layer of kohl around her eyes. She stepped back and smoothed her top over her short skirt knowing she was only delaying the inevitable. She stared into the mirror and looked at her reflection.

"You can do this. Just find out what she wants and warn her off…for the last time." She picked up her bag and left through the back door to avoid the pair out front. She had one stop to make before she met the woman she refused to acknowledge as her mother. Jack and his girlfriend were the least of her worries.

By the time she'd left the post office and pushed the sealed envelope deep into her bag, Sienna's mood had moved to an icy calm. Once and for all she would ensure that Marjorie left them alone and didn't upset Georgie again. She was tough herself, but Georgie got hurt every time Marjorie came back into their lives. Georgie with her happily-ever-after outlook never gave up hoping that their mother would change and would one day want to be a real part of their lives. Having a mother who used people and had no love for her own children had taught Sienna a good lesson in life. Over the years she'd made sure she relied only on herself and needed no one else. Marjorie's arrival after she succumbed to Jack's charm was a timely reminder that she'd been heading to a place she didn't want to be.

Ever. With anyone

She walked down the three steps into the sunken courtyard of the coffee shop and looked around. She dug her huge dark glasses out of her bag and dropped them over her eyes as she walked over to the table at the edge of the garden where Marjorie was sitting.

At least she's by herself. A couple of times over the years she'd arrived with the current boyfriend in tow. The chair scraped on the rough cobblestones when Sienna pulled it away to the side and sat down.

"So how much this time?" She stared through her dark glasses at the woman she had never known as a mother. Marjorie had her head down and was shredding a tissue to bits with shaking fingers.

"I don't want any money."

"That's a change." Sienna kept her voice cold. She was not going to get emotional, and she was not going to show any reaction. The minutes ticked away in an uncomfortable silence and Sienna waited for the inevitable. She knew the pattern.

God, how many times have we sat through this same scenario? No matter how tough she was, Sienna knew she was a soft touch. Keeping their mother in money meant she'd never saved as much as she could have. She'd kept just enough aside for the gallery deposit and her exhibition.

Finally, Marjorie looked up and held her gaze. "I want to tell you something, and I want you to listen without interrupting." Her voice was quavering, and she cleared her throat as she dabbed the tissue to her lips.

Sienna sat back and folded her arms, ignoring the curiosity that tugged at her. "Make it quick. That's my boss who's minding the gallery."

"I thought it was your own business?"

"Ah. So that's the way the land lies." Sienna knew she was being an utter bitch, but she couldn't help it. She had learned how to protect herself from hurt growing up, and she'd do anything to make sure she kept Georgie that way too. There was too much history and too much hurt to be civil to this woman. As far as she was concerned, Marjorie was not her mother.

She looked down in surprise when Marjorie reached across and grabbed her fingers in a death grip. Her thin hand held Sienna's tightly on the tabletop; her sharp nails pressed into Sienna's skin.

"Listen to me. Please? One last time and then I'll leave you in peace. For good." Marjorie's voice broke and Sienna pushed away the sympathy that began to well in her chest.

"I'm ill and I wanted you to hear the truth from me before…before it's too late. It's not right that Renzo has to tell you."

"Tell me what?"

Marjorie kept the tight grip on her hand as though she knew Sienna would get up and leave. It was tempting, but this time, she was going to finish with Marjorie once and for all.

"You're his daughter."

"What?" Sienna's world spun. "Are you crazy? He's my uncle, your brother. He can't be my father."

"It's true. I'm not your birth mother, but Renzo *is* your father."

"You're lying." Sienna reached into her bag with her free hand and pulled out the envelope before shoving it across the table. "I don't know what you're playing at, but I've had enough. There's money in here. I want you to take it and take your silly stories away and leave Georgie and me alone for good. That's it." She fought to keep her voice strong as the thoughts whirled around her head. "That's all I have, and it's worth giving to you to make you go away. I want nothing more to do with you and your crazy ramblings. Do you understand me?"

"Georgie is my child."

Sienna stared at her and let her hand and the envelope drop to the table as the significance of Marjorie's words hit her. For the first time, Marjorie had her attention.

"What are you saying?" Her voice came as a whisper and she pulled her hand out of Marjorie's grasp.

"What can I get you to drink?" The voice of the waitress was a welcome return to normality as she placed a bottle of water and two glasses on the table.

"Coffee, black." Sienna's voice was clipped. She pulled her hand from Marjorie's and poured herself a glass of water and wasn't surprised to see her hand shaking. What Marjorie said was a lie; it had to be.

But why?

Sienna drank deeply and looked up as the waitress turned to Marjorie with a curious glance, but the older woman shook her head and dabbed at the tears on her cheeks.

"Nothing, thank you." Marjorie waited until the waitress had walked to the next table.

"Over the holidays Renzo and I worked in the night harvest in the vineyards in the Hunter Valley. I met Georgie's father there." Her voice was quiet, and she lifted her head and held Sienna's gaze steadily. "I was friends with one of the other girls and she and Renzo had a fling before he came back home." She took a deep breath.

"And…" Sienna prompted her. "What are you trying to tell me?"

"Catherine discovered she was pregnant when she went back home to Tamworth, and she contacted me. When I told her that Renzo was about to get married to Lucia, she decided not to tell him she was having his child."

"I'm not following you. What are you telling me?" Sienna's world was crumbling, and she fought for control, gripping her hands together on her lap. "This sounds like something from a soap opera."

"My friend Catherine was your mother."

"Was? Where is she?" Her voice felt as though it was coming from someone else.

"She got sick when you were only a few weeks old."

Sienna watched as Marjorie shifted her eyes to the envelope on the table. "She came to see me when we were living in Sydney. It was the same week that Georgie's father was leaving to work in the mines. Catherine had put Renzo's name on the birth certificate and when she found out how sick she was, she wanted him to know he had a daughter." She lifted her head. "You."

"But what about Georgie? If this is the truth why did…Uncle Renzo…take us both in? Are you telling me we're not twins?"

Marjorie reached out again, but Sienna kept her hands gripped together. "You *are* cousins, and you share a birthday. You were born on the same day. When Catherine knew she was dying, she asked me to take you, but I wouldn't. I wasn't coping with Georgie, so Renzo and Lucia took you both. She gave them her blessing."

Sienna put her elbows on the table and dropped her head into her hands. It all made sense…sort of. All her life, she'd thought she and Georgie were so different because they were fraternal twins. A small bus pulled up outside and a group of tourists wandered into the courtyard, and their chatter washed over Sienna. She lifted her head and watched them choose a table.

"I followed Georgie's father to Western Australia. I was never very maternal. I knew if he went without me, I'd never see him again. He was the love of my life." Marjorie looked up when the waitress put Sienna's coffee on the table and filled her glass up. "Thank you."

"How do I know I can believe you?" A slow burn was beginning in her stomach, and she took a deep breath as the tears ached at the back of her eyes. She never cried and she wasn't about to start now. It was a sign of weakness, and she was always the strong one.

Marjorie opened her purse and pulled out a folded piece of paper and slid it across the table. "Your birth certificate." She smiled sadly. "I've watched both you and Georgie grow up and I knew you'd need proof. You are a very strong woman, just like Catherine was. She would have been proud of you."

Sienna looked at the paper sitting in front of her as though it would strike and bite her fingers if she touched it. Slowly she reached out, picked it up, and unfolded it. The lines began to waver as Marjorie's words were confirmed by the text in front of her. "What about Georgie? I don't understand. How could you have left her?"

"That's between Georgie and me."

"No." Sienna's control came rushing back. "You're not to tell her. I know my *sister*. She'll be devastated."

Chapter Sixteen

The cool sand squeaked beneath Sienna's bare feet. She walked toward the big tree stump at the top of the beach at the end of Hastings Street; it was surrounded by a few short trees and was private. She dropped her bag and her shoes to the sand and sat on the smooth timber, staring out over the crashing waves. Despite the cool wind, she could barely feel the chill on her arms; her skin was hot and burning. She sat there for a long time staring out to sea as the wind flicked her short hair into spikes around her face. Her whole life had just shifted, and she was numb inside and out.

She kicked at the sand with her toes. *Aunt Marjorie.* Her life savings had extracted the promise that she wouldn't tell Georgie, and she hoped she could trust her. The time had sped by as Sienna had listened to her whole story, and now she glanced at her watch. She'd left the coffee shop and headed straight to the beach, the one place that always managed to soothe her. The way she felt at the moment, she didn't even care if she ever saw the gallery again. It was surreal, and she had to overcome this confusion filling her. She had to come to terms with the thought that Renzo was her father...and her own mother was dead.

The two unexpected visitors today had brought her to her senses. She'd been getting sucked in by her feelings for Jack. Okay, sleeping with him had been fun, but it wasn't going anywhere. Seeing Marjorie had firmed her resolve. Irrespective of the gallery—and the girlfriend—Marjorie reminded her why she didn't do relationships She needed no one in her life. The hollow feeling in her chest and the tears pricking at the backs of her eyelids had nothing to do with regret.

And I have to decide what to tell Georgie.

But first she had to go back to work and tell Jack her exhibition was canned. And she had to face him after last night and probably be in the company of his girlfriend. Giving everything to Marjorie to get rid of her had been worth it and Sienna didn't regret it. Even though it now meant she couldn't afford to pay the costs of holding her exhibition, and any thought of building a studio onto her house had disappeared with the money Marjorie slipped into her bag. She needed time and space to get her thoughts in order. And face Jack. The devastation that tugged at Sienna as her dreams crumbled around her was put away in a deep place where she wouldn't think about it until she had to.

***

Jack turned the closed sign over on the gallery door. He couldn't wait for Sienna to come back. She'd said an hour and she'd already been gone for more than two. He'd managed to convince Arielle that she'd wasted a trip—he ran his hand through his hair and shook his head. He couldn't believe she'd come all the way from Melbourne. He'd booked her on a flight from Brisbane tonight, despite her protests that he'd change his mind about their little misunderstanding.

The look on Sienna's face when he'd walked into the gallery this afternoon had been as cold as ice. Once he told Sienna that Arielle wasn't his girlfriend, maybe they could take up where they'd left off last night. But first he had to get Arielle back to Brisbane. He'd arranged for a bus, but he had to get her to the depot at Caloundra first, and they had to go on his bike.

"Are you ready?" He glanced at her sitting primly on the love seat by the door. "Your luggage will be sent from your hotel to the airport." All he wanted to do was get her on a plane…today.

The spoiled-girl pout was back. "Helen said you'd be pleased to see me." Arielle had always lived in a dream world. He knew his mother would not have encouraged her.

"Helen was wrong. Come on, we've just got time to meet the bus."

###

An hour later, Arielle was safely deposited in the bus on the way to Brisbane Airport. She wasn't happy, but Jack was sure he'd managed to convince her she'd wasted her time. A pleasant tingle ran over his skin as he rode along the short street to the gallery. He'd expected to see the lights on in the gallery, but the building was locked and almost in darkness. Only the soft display lighting in the front was on. He gunned the motor and turned the bike toward home. It seemed like hours since Sienna had been in his arms this morning, and he needed to talk to her and convince her that they…that they could what?

Jack frowned to himself as he turned the bike toward Lake Weyba. They could have a relationship? Or they could just work and play together? He had a feeling Sienna was going to be hard to convince of anything. And the hardest part was he didn't really know what he was trying to convince her that they had between them. Look how Arielle had tried to complicate his life. Maybe he needed to think a bit more and pull back a little?

The house was in darkness too, and he let himself in quietly, heading to the apartment wondering where Sienna was. She'd probably been pissed off with him when she'd come back from her lunch with that woman and found the gallery closed up. But, damn it, it was his business and he could do what he liked with it. His stomach grumbled, adding to his feeling of being out of sorts with the world. He'd go for a run around the lake and then grab some dinner and hit the sack. Maybe she'd come home before then and they could talk.

He pulled on his running shorts and shoes and locked the door behind him as he took off at a slow pace toward the water. There was a distinct chill in the air and winter was not far away. His thoughts ran around his mind and Jack wished he'd thought to grab his iPod so he could listen to music and clear his head.

When did things get so complicated?

Jack narrowed his eyes and peered through the dim light as he headed back toward the house after doing a circuit of the small lake. The light reflected on the small garage at the side of the house and he caught the flash of chrome. Sienna's car was there, but the house was dark. Maybe she'd been picked up? After all, he knew little about her life. But as he ran closer to the house, he saw the flicker of a candle on the back porch. He let out his breath in a sigh of relief, and anticipation filled him.

He grabbed both sides of the stair rail and pulled himself up the four steps leading to the porch as he levelled his breathing. Sienna was curled up in one of the rockers beneath the covered side of the porch, the flickering candle flame the only movement. For a moment he thought she was asleep, but as soon as his shoes hit the wooden decking, she unfolded herself from the chair, stood, and stretched, reaching for a pair of running shoes.

A tight black T-shirt almost reached the top of a pair of black leggings, and he caught a glimpse of bare skin as she raised her arms above her head.

"Great timing," she said. "I was just going to go for a run myself. Cool out there?"

Jack caught his breath, not so much from the exertion but from the cute picture filling his vision.

"Yeah, cool. But it's great by the water once you warm up."

Sienna tied her laces and stood. Jack's breath caught in his throat and he chose his words carefully. "Are we…are you okay?"

"Yes, why do you ask? I'm good. Are you?" Sienna's voice was soft and muffled.

"Whoa." Jack hurried across the porch to catch her, and gently took her arm before she could step down the stairs. "You sound like you're catching a cold. Maybe a run's not such a good idea?" Her skin was icy beneath his fingers. "How about I make you a hot drink? I make a mean lemon hot toddy if you've got a sore throat."

Sienna pulled away from him and bent, stretching her legs. "Thanks, I'm fine. I'm looking forward to a run. I need some fresh air."

"Want some company?" He didn't want to go inside alone. If it meant going for another run, so be it. He could pull the stamina from somewhere.

A slight smile crossed Sienna's face. "Are you up to it?"

The challenge gave Jack a burst of energy. "Of course I am. Are you?"

"Race you to the other side of the lake?" Before he could take another breath, Sienna shot past him, down the steps, and across the small patch of lawn. By the time Jack reached the bottom of the steps, she was opening the gate that led to the narrow path beside the lake. She shot a glance at him and her low chuckle pleased him.

By the time he was through the gate, she was ahead of him and had passed the next two houses along the lake. No way was he going to let her beat him, so Jack took a deep breath and stepped up his pace.

To his surprise, Sienna lengthened the distance between them, and he had to push himself to close the distance. The muscles in his calves burned and he smiled as he almost caught up to her.

"How far are we going?" he huffed as he drew closer to her.

As soon as he spoke, Sienna took off and the distance between them grew again.

"Eat my dust." Her laugh broke the silence of the night. Jack swallowed and gave it all he had.

By the time she'd reached the last house on the other side of the lake, he was right behind her. Her ragged breath as she pushed to the end showed him how determined she had been to beat him.

Sienna grabbed the rail of the jetty of the last house before the path ended in thick trees. She turned with a grin. Jack reached her, rested his arms on the rail, bent over, and tried to catch his breath. Finally, when he could talk, he straightened. Sienna was leaning nonchalantly against the fence, her breathing even and slow, her face slightly pink.

He shook his head with a wry grin. "You didn't even break a sweat."

"Out of shape, Jack?" She smiled back at him and then turned away. "Race you back?"

"Whoa, right there." He reached out and grabbed her arm. "You've made your point. You're fitter than me and you can run like the wind."

"And I feel so much better for it, too." It was great to see the smile on her face as she held his gaze. He pulled her closer and looked down into her eyes. "I'm sorry about today. It wasn't what it looked like."

"What wasn't?" Her eyes narrowed and he realised that even though he had been so worried about her take on Arielle, she seemed to not know that he was talking about it. She stood straight in the loose circle of his arms and looked up at him, her eyes shining in the soft moonlight.

"I want to explain to you…about Arielle."

She lifted her head, and he narrowed his eyes as his gaze settled on her face. At a closer look, her face was pale despite her exertion, and her eyes were slightly puffy. If he didn't know better, he'd swear she'd been crying.

Jack wanted to see her smile again. Frustration warred with wanting to pull her close and kiss her senseless. "Last night was wonderful, and Arielle's arrival was totally unexpected." He waited for her reaction.

A yawn escaped her lips and Jack let his shoulders relax.

"So, I'm boring you now?" he said.

"We didn't get much sleep last night," she said with a slight turning up of her lips.

He grinned, pleased the tension that was swirling between them was easing, and let his gaze settle on her. Dressed all in black, she looked even tinier than normal. She usually gave off an impression of strength, but despite the exertion of the race between them, an air of fragility hung around her tiny shoulders.

He closed his eyes for a moment, remembering the feel of her fine bones beneath his fingers last night. When he opened them, she was looking at him and he was sure she could read his mind.

"I didn't know Arielle was coming to see me, and I want to make one thing quite clear.

She isn't my girlfriend, or my partner, or whatever she told you"

"It's all right, Jack." She stepped away, reached down and stretched one leg. "You don't owe me any explanations. Last night was fun and we got that out of our systems. Now we go back to the way we were. I don't care about Arielle, whatever she is…or was…to you."

"But you look—" He didn't want to say that she looked upset because it sounded as though he was an arrogant jerk, as though she cared enough to be upset by Arielle arriving. She'd made it quite clear from the outset that there was going to be nothing between them. Maybe something else was wrong? He'd give her some time and if she wanted to talk, he'd be there to listen.

"You look tired. And so am I." He pushed himself from the rail and held out his hand. "Okay, race you back."

Sienna grinned at him and stepped onto the path.

"Sienna?"

She stopped and looked back at him "Yes?"

"Your shoelace is undone."

She crouched down in the darkness and by the time she realised both her laces were intact Jack had taken off and was twenty yards ahead of her.

With a grin, he called back over his shoulder. "Gotcha."

The sound of her laughter behind him sent a warm feeling rushing through his chest.

Chapter Seventeen

Sienna slept deeply despite the crazy dreams of weddings where Renzo was giving her away. In her dreams, she walked down an aisle over and over, hanging on to his arm, but when she got to the front there was no one there. She was alone in the church and even Renzo had disappeared.

Runaway groom phobias. Something she'd never have to worry about. It must be the thought of her mother deciding not to tell Renzo about his child when she first fell pregnant—about *her*—and Arielle that had gotten her mind spinning.

Sienna stood beneath the shower and let the warm water run down her face and neck. She always did her best thinking in the shower, or by the beach, but today her thoughts whirled around, and she couldn't come to a decision. Closing her eyes, she leaned her head back and wished that the water could wash away all of her problems.

Marjorie had sworn that she wouldn't tell Georgie what she had told Sienna yesterday. Sienna knew that she couldn't trust her not to tell Georgie, so she was going to have to make time to see her tonight. Taking time out wasn't a problem anymore; her exhibition was going to be canned and there was no need to work on the enamelling every night. Her throat ached with the disappointment of her lost dream, and Sienna gave in to the tears and let them fall until she was drained. She had worked toward that dream for two years, and in one afternoon, it was all gone.

Along with my money. Maybe she'd been foolish, but she wanted to protect Georgie and ensure that she was the one to break the news. She knew that Georgie would be hit hard by the revelation that they weren't twins…or even sisters. Sienna tipped her head back and let the warm water wash away her tears. She couldn't cope with the knowledge either, but she knew she would have to learn to accept it.

She would have a busy day ahead, and she'd tell Jack he could have the studio as soon as he wanted it. Making the call to the newspaper to pull the ad, and cancelling the catering, would fill in some of the day.

###

Fifteen minutes later, she was dressed and sitting in her car—her dead car—as the damn motor refused to fire. Taking it to the mechanic had slipped her mind over the past couple of days.

"Problems?" Jack stood at the front of the bumper bar, his hands on his hips, his jeans slung low on his waist, and his chest bare as it seemed to be more often than not. Sienna's mouth dried and she tore her gaze away. Racing with Jack last night had done her good. He'd seemed genuinely worried about her being upset, and that had touched her, but she hadn't wanted to go into explanations of what was bothering her. They'd had fun and she had appreciated his thoughtfulness. Plus, she'd enjoyed beating him to the other side of the lake. If he hadn't tricked her, she would have beaten him back. She'd run that path so many times she could have done it in her sleep.

"Blasted car. I forgot to call the mechanic."

And I won't be able to for a while now that I've cleaned out my bank account.

She opened the door and eased herself out and avoided looking at Jack's bare chest as he moved closer to her. Turning the key in the door, she locked it and stepped back and began to count.

"One, two, three—"

"What are you doing? Trying to keep your temper intact?" Jack's roguish grin interrupted her counting and Sienna pursed her lips and waved her arm at him.

"Four, five, six, seven, eight, nine…ten!" She unlocked the door and sat in the driver's seat. "I'm trying something."

Jack crossed his arms, watching her with an intent expression as he leaned against the side of the carport while she put the key in the ignition and turned it. The engine purred to life and she looked at him with a grin.

"It worked!"

"The counting? Was it overheated?" Jack stepped forward and crouched beside the car, and his face was close enough that she could see the gold flecks in his green eyes.

"No, I was experimenting." Sienna let the rush of pleasure flow though her as she looked at him. She was feeling very clever…and very relieved. "Before I had my iPad, I had a clunky old PC and every time it jammed, I used to shut it down, count to ten, and restart it. It always worked like a charm. I thought I'd test the theory on my BMW. After all, it has a computer system…I think?"

Jack burst out laughing and Sienna ignored the tremble that ran down to her fingertips. "I'd still take it to a mechanic and get it checked out."

"I will…when I get time," she said. "Are you coming into the gallery today?"

His gaze shifted from hers and he shook his head. "No, I thought I'd look around for a place to live. I'll move into the studio if I haven't found anything after your exhibition."

Sienna reached out and put her hand over his. "I was hoping you'd come in today because I wanted to discuss my plans with you."

"Your plans?"

"Yes, I've had a…er…a change of direction."

"And…" Jack raised his brows in question.

Might as well get it out of the way now.

"I'm postponing my exhibition." She couldn't bring herself to say cancelling. When he went to speak, she interrupted. "I don't want to rush it. When I hold it, I want it all to be just right, and I've left it too late to give it my best work. So there's no hurry for me to finish my work. You can start using the studio as soon as you want to."

That sounded better than saying I gave all my money to my scheming aunt and I can't afford it now.

"No, you can't do that," Jack shook his head. "I'll come in today and we can talk about it. If you're running out of time, I'll help out. I'll hire someone else to work in the gallery while you get your pieces ready. And don't worry, I'll still pay you."

A sweet feeling of gratitude rushed through her and she squeezed his fingers. He really was a nice guy, but it was too late. "That's really kind of you, but I've made up my mind. I'm not ready. In a few months, I'll be in a better place."

"A better place? You're leaving the gallery?" Jack's brow wrinkled in a frown.

"No, I meant a better place personally." As soon as the words were out, Sienna bit her lip. *Shit*, she hadn't meant to say that. "I haven't decided about the gallery. Apart from deciding to postpone my exhibition."

"Personally? You *are* upset about the other night. Or was it Arielle turning up?" Jack's intent gaze was seeing way too much, and she lifted her fingers from his and put the car into gear.

"Nothing for you to worry about." She let off the handbrake and waited for him to stand up. "I'll see you later, then. Okay?"

"Okay. Have a good day. I'll call in later." Jack waved as she backed the car from the carport, and Sienna let out the breath she'd been holding. The sooner she sorted out her private life, and the sooner she decided what she was going to do about her job, the better it would be for all concerned. So much had happened in the last week, she needed to get away. As soon as Faith's birthday party was over…and she'd spoken to Georgie, she was going to take some time for herself.

Chapter Eighteen

After Sienna turned from the drive and the last flash of red sports car disappeared through the trees, Jack walked back inside. The place felt empty without her. He flicked on the coffeemaker and drew a deep breath as her perfume lingered in the kitchen.

I've got it bad.

And he felt bad. Despite what she said, he knew Sienna was upset because they'd spent the night together, and then Arielle flitted in the next morning.

Something else was bugging her.

One minute they'd been laughing and joking and sharing a great night in bed together. Now she'd canned her exhibition and was talking about moving on, when all he wanted to do was take her in his arms and try to make it up to her. He'd been in knots wondering how he was going to take over the studio and leave her without somewhere to work. He thought he'd wanted to date Sienna and have some fun, without living and working in the same place…now he couldn't bear to be away from her. When she was away from him, the light went out of his day. Hell, he'd even put in a day's work at the gallery if it meant spending more time with her.

What was wrong with him?

A few days away was what he needed. He'd committed to going to Faith's birthday party and was looking forward to catching up with them.

Especially Blake.

Maybe a game of golf and catching up with his mate would help him sort his head out. Blake and Ana and Sienna seemed to be great friends. Maybe it wasn't Arielle showing up that had turned her cold toward him. He shrugged; it wasn't any of his business. The week after the party, he'd jump on the bike and head down the coast and visit some of his mates down there. Then he'd come back, move into a new place, and get to work on his sculptures.

Here, in my *studio.* He didn't need to be around her.

It was so out of character for him to be worrying about things out of his control. He needed to chill and get his head back together.

He wandered through the apartment with his coffee and looked out the window over the lake. Despite being here such a short time, he felt right at home in this place, and it was going to be hard to move out. Maybe if he offered the right money, he could talk Sienna into selling it to him, especially if she decided to move on to another gallery or back up the coast. But if she did, he'd miss her, and he really hoped she'd choose to stay on at the Sea View Gallery.

He picked up his cell and dialled Blake's number. No time like the present.

"Jack! How's it going?" Blake's voice was upbeat as usual. Since he'd settled in the Sunshine Coast hinterland, Blake had unwound, and the uptight executive had changed into a laidback husband and father

"Hey, mate. I was wondering if you had time for a game of golf in your busy schedule?"

"Maybe. When were you planning to come up and play?"

"How about I stay up there and we get together the day after the birthday party?" Jack grinned.

"Sounds like a plan. How's the gallery going?" Blake's tone was bland.

"Hidden subtext? You mean how are Sienna and I getting along?"

"Yeah, I thought you might have some issues there." Blake laughed. "She's the toughest of the three girls. I wondered how things were going down there with you two. Ana hasn't spoken to her for a few days."

"We're getting on very well. She's a great person. She's a talented artist and she's done a great job with the gallery in the short time she's been here. And her house is amazing."

"Still smitten, then?"

"No, we have a business relationship, that's all. You know me, I don't mix business and pleasure." A little white lie, but it wasn't the right thing to share, even with a good mate.

"But you've been out to her place?"

"I'm actually living in her apartment—"

"You always were a fast mover."

"I'm taking it slow." That's as much as Jack was going to say.

"I've got some news for you, Jack. This golf game will be the last for a while. Ana and

I are moving back to Melbourne for a year. I'm helping your dad out for a few months."

"How come? I thought you loved it up here?" A twinge of guilt was quickly pushed away. Dad knew he wasn't coming back, so getting Blake back to Melbourne was a good move. He was just surprised that Blake had agreed to go.

"Won't be for long. Ana was hoping you'd look out for Sienna a bit."

"I think she's pretty good at looking out for herself."

"That's the front she puts up, but she's as soft as butter beneath that." Blake's voice was protective. "But hey, listen. Don't hurt her, okay? She's a special lady."

Ah, maybe Ana moving away was what had upset Sienna? Jack wanted to get off the call so he could think things through a bit more. "Listen, I'm just on my way out. I'll see you at the party."

"Looking forward to it. Never thought I'd end up a doting dad and husband. Lot to be said for it, Jack."

"Not for me, mate. See you soon." He disconnected the call and headed for the shower. It was time to go and find a place to live before he got too settled in here.

***

By the middle of the morning, Sienna had cancelled all of the arrangements for the exhibition and taken down the posters from the window of the gallery. All she had to do was go for a walk and get the posters taken down in the post office and the few shops that had agreed to put them up for her around Noosa. And she'd taken a call from Katy, the new gallery assistant, saying she had a job in Brisbane and wouldn't be able to help out. She'd close at lunchtime, unless Jack came in to look after the gallery.

She swallowed hard and leaned back against her chair; regret spiked her chest. She'd have her show one day. For the first time since she'd moved to Noosa, Sienna looked around the gallery and thought of moving on. Maybe she would sell her house to Jack. Ever since Marjorie had dropped the truth on her, she'd found it hard to get motivated, and she even wondered for the first time if she was kidding herself thinking she could be a successful artist.

The pieces on the shelves glowed beneath the soft light, and she watched as a couple of tourists admired the display across the room. Her work here was done, and it was time to think about where she was going. In one way, Marjorie had done her a favour and pushed her to make the decision about the gallery—and Jack—more quickly. Sienna knew she had to get away, because he was altogether too damned sexy, and it would only be a matter of time before she gave in to what she wanted. Getting involved with him was too complicated. There were so many things she didn't like about him. He was too laidback and casual about this business, he'd lied to her about being an artist, and…

But if she was honest, she knew she was stretching it, because she was so damned attracted to him. She wasn't going to get involved with anyone. She was keeping her heart intact from now on. Relationships were not for her. Not with anyone. Not with him.

Him. Jack.

And she intended to keep her life private and her emotions safe.

Sienna touched the screen of her iPad and opened a browser window. Her fingers hovered over the touch-screen keyboard, until she drew a deep breath and typed in the words "Catherine Elizabeth Stuart, Tamworth." She'd looked at the birth certificate so many times, it was almost falling to pieces.

Tears filled her eyes. Of course the first damn search result pulled up her mother's name and her dates of birth and death. Nothing was private these days. You could Google just about anything, but the last thing Sienna had expected to see was her mother's life dates on the screen in front of her. Her vision blurred as she ran her finger down the screen and read the funeral notice that had obviously been scanned in from a funeral home. She checked the website; it was archived newspaper issues scanned and indexed as a part of a local history project for an ancestry database. She emailed the page to the printer and put the iPad aside as a customer wandered over with a small vase in her hand.

Brushing her eyes with the back of her hand, Sienna greeted the lady with a smile. "You've chosen a lovely piece."

She still had a job to do.

###

Jack wandered in mid-afternoon. She'd closed the gallery at noon and visited the shops to take down the ads. The disappointment expressed by the locals that her show had been postponed had lifted her, one of the best things that happened to her this week.

Almost the best.

Her thoughts went straight back to the night with Jack in the studio. Nothing could compare to that. She pushed away the thought, and because she was trying to block it out, her voice was short when she greeted him

"I'm about to close."

"That's fine. I came in to take you for dinner before you go home."

Sienna's head flew up. "Why?"

"Because you look like you need cheering up…and I wanted to convince you I'm a nice guy."

Tears pricked her eyes again. She'd been so damn emotional since Marjorie had dropped the news on her, she was tearing up at stupid things, and it wasn't the way she usually dealt with problems. Not by a long shot.

Turning away so he couldn't see her eyes fill, Sienna slid her iPad into its case. "There's no need for that. I told you last night what you do has nothing to do with me."

"Okay, how about we go to dinner and talk about why you've cancelled your show."

"No." Sienna put her iPad in the drawer beneath the desk and shut it with a firm push. The tiny desk rocked on its narrow legs, and Jack grabbed for the antique lamp that teetered on the corner at the same time she did. Their fingers brushed and she pulled back when her skin tingled.

"Whoa, that was close." He lifted the lamp and put it closer to the middle of the desk.

"Thank you."

"Okay, third and final try. One, I don't need to explain Arielle to you?"

"No."

"Two, you don't want to talk about your exhibition?"

"No." Sienna glanced up at him from beneath her lashes, and her breath caught in her throat. She bit down the beginning of a smile that was playing around her mouth as Jack got down on to his knees.

"Three." He put his hands together in front of his chest and Sienna let the smile spread.

"Three?" she asked.

"I want to go back to that fantastic Italian restaurant, and I hate eating alone, and I enjoy your company. Is that enough?"

For the first time since she'd raced him last night, a laugh bubbled up from Sienna's chest and she let it out past her lips. "You are one very persuasive man, Jack."

"And a hungry one. So, dinner?" He pushed to his feet and crooked his arm and held it out to her."

Sienna stared at his arm as a breathless feeling radiated throughout her chest. She had an inkling she was making a big mistake, but she guessed she had to eat. She would go and see Georgie tomorrow.

"How about a compromise? Instead of going all the way to Coolum, there's a nice little Italian restaurant around the corner." She pressed her lips tightly together, so she didn't look too enthusiastic, and ignored Jack's arm when she glanced at her watch. "And you do realise it's not dinnertime yet?"

"I can wait." He grinned at her. "I might have to grab a burger to see me through, but I'll look forward to Italian. Are you going home first?"

She shook her head. "No, I was going to close up here and do some accounts."

"Don't work too hard. I'll come back at six. Okay?"

Her gaze met his and held it for a long moment, and Sienna knew she'd made the wrong call. Spending more time in Jack's company than she had to was going to put her emotions in the way of logical—and safe—decision-making.

I don't need this. But the warmth filling her chest belied her thoughts.

She'd make certain they would have a quick meal, and then she'd go home and get a good night's sleep.

By myself.

Things would look better in the morning. *They would.*

Chapter Nineteen

"Sienna!" Giuseppe, the owner of the small Italian restaurant near the beach at Noosa, gathered her into a tight hug. "We haven't seen you here for a long time. How is your Uncle Renzo? I must go up to Maleny and beat him in a game of bocce. He owes me a game."

Sienna swallowed and tried to keep her composure when Giuseppe mentioned…her father. It brought the events of the last few days crashing back. She put her hand on the back of the chair to steady herself and forced a cheerful smile onto her face. "I haven't been to see him for a few weeks, but I'll let him know you're after a rematch when I'm"—she glanced at Jack— "we're up there next weekend."

She stepped to the side as Jack pulled her chair out for her, and Giuseppe opened the napkin with a dramatic flourish.

"Now, you must have the spaghetti marinara tonight." Once Sienna was seated and he'd laid the napkin on her lap, he put his fingers to his lips in a very Italian gesture. "*Delizioso.* The seafood is fresh off the boat this morning." His chest puffed out and he smiled before he walked back to the kitchen; a pang of nostalgia ran through Sienna. She missed her friends in Maleny. Apart from Ana and Georgie, they were all older folks, and many were Italians whose family had settled on the coastal fringe and worked in the sugar industry a couple of generations back. In one way she was looking forward to going back home to Faith's birthday party, but she was dreading seeing Renzo. She glanced up at Jack, who'd settled in the chair across from her. She knew the tongues would wag when he turned up at the party. Thelma and Mitzi would be in matchmaking heaven. They'd taken full credit for Blake and Ana's blissful state of matrimony, totally ignoring the fact that they'd known each other since college.

"Penny for your thoughts?"

Sienna jumped as Jack's words broke through the happy background noise of the restaurant. "I was thinking about Montville. You're still coming to Faith's party?"

"Of course. I'm not going to let my Prince Charming tights go to waste." Jack grinned at her, and that ever-present warmth that filled her whenever she was near him spread a little further. "And I'm golfing with Blake on Monday."

"So you're not going to come back and open the gallery the day after the party. Did you get my message about taking time off?" She'd sent him an email about taking time off, and about Katy, but he hadn't replied.

"No, I haven't checked." Jack held her gaze as he picked up the water carafe and filled her glass.

Of course he hadn't.

"That's fine. Whatever suits you. You're the boss. I might just close the gallery for a few days."

"No, Jack. *You're* the boss. I'm the manager." His casual attitude really got under her skin at times. For the life of her she still couldn't understand why he'd bought the place. It would have been easier to buy a regular studio space. He said he wanted nothing to do with running a business and having any responsibility, but sometimes she sensed it was an act he put on. No one could be that relaxed and carefree all the time.

Could they?

"So you don't check your email either?"

He shrugged. "I got fed up with email when I was working for the company when Dad was sick. People expect you to jump immediately just because they can send you an email any time of the day or night."

Sienna held his gaze and watched him. He leaned back casually in his chair and looked at her, but it was hard to see what he was thinking.

"I check it once a day." He sounded a little defensive. Great, she'd gotten under his skin. It felt good to get a reaction out of him. She decided to push a little harder.

It was as good a time as any to tell him she'd come to a decision. "I might as well tell you now. I've decided to leave at the end of the month, so if you're not interested in the gallery yourself, you'd better start looking for another manager." Sienna sipped her water and looked over the rim of the glass at him.

Jack steepled his fingers beneath his chin and stared back at her. The grin had left his face and his eyes were hooded. "You've made up your mind. I can't persuade you to stay?"

Sienna held his gaze and shook her head, still wondering if she'd made the wrong decision. Now that she'd put it into words, she'd have to stick with it.

"Where are you going?" His voice was soft, and she leaned forward to hear.

"I don't know. I've got some things I need to do. I might travel for a while."

"Shit, Sienna." Jack's voice held a rough edge. "You sure know how to make a guy feel bad. Where did all this come from? A few days ago, you were on a path to buying the gallery and having your first show." He reached across to take her hand, but she pulled it away and clenched it in her lap as he kept talking.

"Changing my mind about selling can't have had such an impact on your decision so quickly?"

For a fleeting moment the perplexed look on Jack's usually happy face, and the concern in his voice, rattled her, and she was tempted to tell him everything that had happened. She opened her mouth, and then she remembered what a laidback guy he was. Would he care? She wasn't going to risk it.

Keep your private business close to your heart. Don't depend on anyone else.

Taking a deep breath, she crossed her arms. "Don't concern yourself. I'm a flighty person, always changing my mind. You probably did me a favour. Just ask the girls next weekend. You can't rely on me."

Jack's eyes hadn't left her face, and she dropped her gaze to her lap, surprised to see her hands were white from clenching them so tightly. She relaxed them and looked back up at him as he leaned forward.

"Well, I hope you change it back again, because you're making the wrong decision based on very little reason."

The anger that shot through her was welcome. She was well and truly sick of feeling sorry for herself, and she lashed out at him. "Oh, do you? And what do you know about me? Do you think one night in my bed—actually it's your bed, isn't it, I keep forgetting—makes you an expert on how I feel and gives you the right to tell me you think I should change my mind back again?"

Jack held up his hand. "There's no need to be so angry."

Regret spiked through her chest. There was no need to take it out on Jack. Even though he drove her crazy with his casual attitude, he *was* too nice a guy to wear her temper. And way too nice for her peace of mind.

"Ignore me. I've been feeling sorry for myself and it's time to get over it." She swallowed and held his green-eyed gaze, trying to ignore the regret that was filling her. Maybe they could have had a relationship if he'd sold her the gallery. Just as well it had turned out the way it had, because she'd been sucked in by him. He'd almost gotten past her resolve of not investing emotionally in a relationship. Marjorie and Arielle had turned up in the nick of time. It would have been a huge mistake.

"I've got some news you might like. I'm selling my house, too. If you're still interested you can have first option on it. It'll save me a lot of time before I head off."

This time she couldn't help the tears that filled her eyes, and she brushed them away angrily before they could spill onto her cheeks.

My job, my exhibition, and my cottage. And worst of all my sister. All from the telling of one truth by the woman she had thought was her mother. Sienna had lost so much in the last few days. She wasn't even going to think about losing what might have been with Jack. She steeled herself and swallowed back her despair

"Now let's order and get out of here as soon as we can. This was a bad idea."

***

Jack felt like a total and absolute heel. His move to Noosa and his decision to keep the gallery—the gallery that he'd had nothing to do with since he'd bought it—had brought a lot of turmoil into Sienna's life. He'd never been able to handle it when a woman cried. Arielle had picked that up mighty quick, and now Sienna was on the verge of tears. But she wasn't ready to fall into his arms to be comforted—she had her hard shell back up and in place.

The silence stretched uncomfortably as their meals were delivered; he ate without tasting anything. Finally, Sienna pushed her plate to the side and held his gaze.

Her eyes were huge and touched by shadows on the fine, transparent skin beneath them. Her cheeks were lightly flushed, and her full lips set in a straight line. A pang of sympathy shot through him, and his fingers itched to reach out and cup her face.

"I've had enough. Can you pay the bill? I'll see you tomorrow." The legs of the chair scraped on the tiled floor with a loud squeak when Sienna pushed it back and rose gracefully to her feet. Her shoulders were stiff, and he sensed she was only just holding herself together.

"I'm sorry. I'm not very good company tonight." Sienna's voice was soft, and she avoided his gaze.

"Wait for me. I'll walk you back." He kept his voice firm. "We need to talk."

Sienna ignored him and strode to the door, giving Giuseppe a wave in the kitchen as she hurried past. Jack pulled out his wallet and threw a hundred-dollar bill to the waitress. "Keep the change." He pushed open the door and looked up the street. She must have run, because she was almost to the corner of the street where the gallery was.

"Wait," he called after her as he took off in a jog. Even without running shoes, she had the key to the front door in her hand by the time he caught up.

"I asked you to wait for me."

"I heard you, and I didn't want to."

Jack took her arm gently. "Sienna, listen to me. We're going to sit down and talk this out."

"I don't want to."

Jack ran his fingers through his hair. "Well, I do." He took the key from her and opened the door with one hand without letting her go with the other. Sienna tried to pull away as he gently led her through the gallery to the studio.

"I'm not going to let you go, or you'll take off."

She glared at him without speaking. At least the tears had gone. They reached the sofa bed, and he sat her down on it before he let go of her arm. He stood in front of the sofa and crossed his arms.

"I've changed my mind." Jack waited for her to look at him after he spoke.

She lifted her head. "About what?" Her face was closed, but at least she was listening to him.

"About the gallery. About the studio." He crouched down in front of her, and the whiff of perfume that reached him pulled him back two nights to when they'd been laughing together in this bed. Jack held her gaze with his. "I've watched you work here, and I know how well you do it. I'm going to contact Dad's secretary and tell her to redo the contract and we'll go ahead with the sale."

She gazed up at him. "You can't do that. What about your commission?"

He waved his hand and grinned. "I'll sort something out. It's not the end of the world if it's a bit late." Surprise shot through him as his words hung in the air. He realised it didn't matter. Sienna's happiness was more important than anything he had to prove to himself…or his father. Or had thought he did. Yeah, he had a deadline, and he wanted to show Dad he wasn't a loser, but none of that mattered. Sienna's happiness was more important to him. His priorities had switched, and he hadn't even been aware of it happening. Money wasn't going to rule his life; if he lost this commission, there would be more.

Her sharp floral perfume washed over him as her eyes lit up, and then her face closed again as she drew her lips together. "I don't want it anymore."

"Sienna, do you know what you want?" As soon as the words left his lips, he regretted them.

Her mouth dropped open as she took a deep breath, and he couldn't keep his eyes off her lips. "Oh, yes, Jack. I do. But what I want, and what's right for me, are not necessarily the same thing."

Goddamn it, he couldn't help himself. His arms seemed to go around her of their own accord and he crushed her against his chest. He dropped his chin to the top of her head as she leaned into him and relaxed. "I'm sorry I've made you so unhappy by coming to Noosa."

He felt her take another deep breath before she pulled away and tipped her head back. "It's okay." Her eyes held his steadily, and a flash of desire shot through him. "It's not you."

"I made the wrong decision in the first place. You've just helped me move forward with some personal issues I have to consider now."

Jack shook his head slowly. "Has it got anything to do with Arielle?"

Sienna stared at him for a moment longer before she reached up and patted his cheek in an almost motherly touch. "No, it hasn't. You're a good man, Jack. You're very kind and thoughtful, but it's too late. You're not as casual and carefree as you try to make out you are."

She moved away from him and stood. "Now, I'm going home. I'll see you tomorrow if you come into the gallery."

Jack rocked back on his heels and watched as she picked up her bag and pulled her car keys out. He didn't follow when she let herself out of the back door. He waited till the throaty purr of her car reached him as she backed out of the parking space. At least it had started.

He stood and dropped onto the soft cushions and inhaled her floral perfume which lingered in the air. The sofa bed was looking good. He couldn't trust himself to stay away from Sienna if he followed her home.

***

Sienna walked into the cold, empty bedroom and threw her bag onto the bed. It landed with a soft *thump* and she crossed to the window. The moon was hidden behind heavy clouds and the night was dark. It suited her mood. Leaving Jack had been hard; when he'd held her, she'd enjoyed the comfort of his arms and tried to ignore the excitement that his touch brought. But the last few days had reinforced her conviction not to let anyone too close—not even Jack, though it was so very tempting to lean on him.

Georgie had hit the nail on the head. "It'll just complicate matters if you have to work for him," she'd said. But neither of them had any idea that Sienna would fall for him. Or what this week would bring.

Admitting to herself that she was falling for him was in a strange way, cathartic, and Sienna felt a bit happier. She turned away from the window and her gaze settled on her cell phone, which must have fallen to the floor when she threw her bag onto the bed. She groaned as she picked it up. She scrolled though over twenty missed texts and calls from Georgie. All thoughts of Jack fled from her mind as her protective instinct kicked in.

"Damn it. Marjorie, if you've told her and broken your word, I'll have my money back." Sienna muttered under her breath as she scrolled though message by message trying to see if Georgie knew the truth.

When Jack said he'd still sell her the gallery, hope had filled her for an instant, before she remembered she'd given Marjorie her life savings. The bank wouldn't approve the business loan without a substantial deposit. Now her bank account was empty, and it looked like giving the money to Marjorie to buy her silence had been a waste of time.

How could I have been so gullible?

She held the phone in her hand and looked at the screen as she tried to decide what to do. There was no decision to be made. She took a deep breath and pressed speed dial for Georgie. She should have gone up to Maleny tonight and not given in to the temptation of being with Jack.

Georgie's voice broke as soon as she answered the call. "No matter what she's done, she can't destroy our relationship. We're still sisters."

"She told you." Sienna fought back the dismay that flooded through her. "What about…have you seen Uncle…Renzo?" she asked. She was still having difficulty coming to terms with him being her father and not her uncle.

"No, but Marjorie said she told him she was going to tell both of us."

"She promised me she wouldn't tell you. I wanted to tell you."

"You don't always have to be the strong one, you know. I'm not as weak as you seem to think."

Tears ached behind Sienna's eyes. "I'm sorry. I just wanted to be there when you found out. After all"—she tried to inject some mirth into her voice to lighten the mood— "I am the oldest.

"You are. But I'm okay. It makes sense, doesn't it?"

Sienna wiped her eyes with the back of her hand. "Yes, it does."

"Are you coming up to see Uncle Renzo?"

"No, and I'm not going to call. I'll see him at Faith's party."

"Love ya, sis. Remember I worry about you, too. You don't have to do all the worry for both of us."

Sienna swallowed. Georgie would be so upset when she heard she'd paid off Marjorie.

They ended the call and Sienna gave way to the tears. She didn't feel very strong at the moment. She wiped her face with the back of her hands; it was time to pull herself together and get on with her life. How could things have changed so much since their birthdays such a short time ago?

###

The rest of the week passed quickly. Sienna avoided Jack on the odd occasion he came into the gallery. Luckily the gallery was busy, and she'd been with customers each time he walked in. He must have been staying in the studio because there'd been no sign of him at the house each night.

Sienna started to clear out the studio; she packed up the frogs and took them home. Her car hadn't let her down again, and she decided it was a glitch she'd ignore. Hopefully it was all right, because she couldn't afford to get it fixed. She straightened her shoulders with a grim smile; she couldn't afford anything, but she was not going to give in to tears.

The gallery was quiet this morning, and there had been no sign of Jack since yesterday. She stared at the display on the shelves in front of her, flicking a duster without really seeing what was in front of her. The conversation with Georgie the other night had been emotional, and she was pleased Jack had given her some space since then. Maybe the situation wasn't going to be too bad. The next hurdle was seeing Renzo—her father. Once she'd done that, she could figure out what was next.

As much as she tried, she couldn't put Jack out of her thoughts. The worst part about the week had been his absence. Even though it had been merely a week, she'd seen him only from a distance and she missed him around the gallery and the house. He was obviously avoiding her, and that was something she was going to have to get over. She'd booked a flight south for the night of Faith's party and she needed to make sure Jack had found someone to look after the place. He couldn't shut it, no matter what he said. That would be bad for business. She typed him an email. They could work out the details on the weekend at the birthday party.

A reluctant smile tugged at her lips. But would he check it?

Chapter Twenty

Sienna leaned closer to the mirror and drew a perfect circle on each cheek before filling it in with bright pink lip gloss. Being an artist and having a steady hand helped with getting into costume. Hopefully, she'd remember to keep her hands away from her face while she was driving up to Maleny. She'd figured it was easier to get dressed in the fairy costume and wear it and carry a change of clothes for the plane in the backpack she packed for her trip. She'd already asked Georgie to take her to the airport.

    Smoothing down the stiff tulle of the short skirt, she pirouetted and grinned at herself in the mirror. She could just see little Faith clapping her hands when the three fairies arrived in costume for her party. The low throb of a motorcycle engine caught her attention and her hands stilled on the skirt of the costume and her heart sped up. She tried to ignore the excited anticipation that curled in her stomach.

I wonder why he's here.

She'd been hoping to see Jack before the party, because she wanted to apologise to him for her moodiness the other night. Now that she was beginning to get used to the bombshell that Marjorie had dropped, her mood had improved, and she was more settled—or had been until she'd heard the deep roar of the motorbike.

She waited for Jack to come through the house, biting her lip as she stood there. She hoped he still felt comfortable enough to come in. A couple of taps at the front door sounded rather than the expected turn of a key she'd waited to hear.

Holding her breath, and with her hands clenched together in front of her, Sienna took one last look in the mirror before she crossed the hall to open the door.

At least the fairy clothes might lighten the situation.

"Wow, a fairy princess."

Sienna held the sides of the tulle skirt and dropped into a little curtsy. Jack's face lit up in a wide grin and a pleasant shiver trembled down her back. If anything, he was more tanned and relaxed than he'd been earlier in the week when he'd last been in the gallery. It was impossible to upset the man. He was always so damned *happy*.

"That's me. What can I do for you, Jack?"

"I'm on my way to the birthday party, but my Prince Charming costume is here."

She stepped back to let him inside.

"I was going to get in my costume when I got there. Maybe I should get changed before I go?"

A little devil poked her as she thought of Jack riding up the highway as Prince Charming. "Definitely. Ana made it quite clear on the invitation that we all arrive in costume."

"Hmm. I'm going to look ridiculous riding up the mountain." His nonchalant grin sent a tremble down her back.

"You are." Sienna smiled at him. She felt so much better now that he'd stopped by. "I'm going straight to the airport after the party." She wasn't going to tell him where she was going. Or why she was going there. He unsettled her enough without adding feeling sorry for her to the mix. She *had* to get over him.

"Okay. The holiday will do you a lot of good. You work too hard." He grinned and her heart went triple time as the sexy crinkles around his eyes deepened.

"Why didn't you use your key?" She followed him down the hall. "You didn't have to knock."

"I thought it was more polite."

"Have you been sleeping in the studio?" If he had, he'd been gone every morning when she'd got there.

"No, I've been staying at a hotel."

Guilt ran through her, and she frowned. "You didn't have to do that."

"No problem. Once you finish up at the gallery, I'll stay in the studio." He stared at her. "You know yourself how convenient it is to work and sleep there."

"Yes, I do." Heat filled her cheeks as she thought of the last time she'd spent the night there. "It's a great space. It's got everything you could need."

The last couple of days had passed in a blur, but the time she'd spent finalising the bookings and the accounts had been hard, especially not knowing where she was going to go after she left here. Every time the phone had rung about her cancelled exhibition, Sienna's confusion deepened, and she was almost—only almost—beginning to regret her quick decision to leave. As far as cancelling the exhibition went, she'd had no choice; she couldn't afford to pay for it now. Once she visited her mother's grave, she was going to find closure and think about her future.

"Sienna?" Jack's voice interrupted her thoughts. "I've parked behind your car. Can you wait until I get changed?"

"Sure, I still have to pack the cakes up."

Jack disappeared into the apartment. "I'll be quick."

Sienna went to the kitchen and transferred the fairy cakes from the fridge to a large container. She hummed a nursery rhyme as she worked; Mitzi and Thelma would be proud of her—a domestic goddess and cook she was not. She stepped back and surveyed her creation. As much detailed work had gone into decorating each cake as she put into her sculptures. Each cake was topped with a couple of little fairy-tale characters in a profusion of bright primary colours.

"They're not for eating, are they?" Jack must have been standing close behind her, because she could feel his breath on her neck. "They're fantastic. Make sure you get a photo of them."

Sienna stepped sideways away from the warmth of his arm when he pointed to the cakes. She walked around to the other side of the table and reached for the lid of the container before leaning across and snapping it shut. "Will you carry…oh my goodness!"

Her hand flew to her mouth to stifle the giggle that threatened to spill over.

With his sun-lightened hair and his tanned face, not to mention the skin-tight costume, Jack made a stunning Prince Charming.

"You like?" He grinned and dropped into a bow. Hot–pink tights encased his long muscular thighs, and a deep green slimline satin top was tucked into the waistband of his tights

"You look like the guy in *Shrek*." She stumbled over the words when heat reached her cheeks; she was grateful for the pink makeup. Every inch of him was outlined by the tights.

"Which one? Not the Mummy's boy one?"

She let the giggle spill out. "Yes, *that* one. I think that's the costume they've sold you."

"But is it okay?"

"Yes, I love it." She lifted her gaze to meet his as her giggle broke into a laugh. "You're not really going to ride your bike like that?" She looked down at the heavy motorcycle boots he held in one hand. "I guess you are."

"It's good to see you smile again, Sienna." He held her gaze. "There's something I want to talk to you about."

No, he sounded way too serious. She ignored his words and the tremble that ran down her back. "You'll certainly attract some attention on the road."

"I've done worse," he said with a sexy grin, and the tremble hit her legs.

It was good to have him back around. She liked the happy way he made her feel but wasn't so sure about the shaky feeling that went with it. "I don't think I need to know."

"Come on. Time to go to the party." He held his free hand out for the cake box. "And we are going to find time for a talk sometime this afternoon before you leave."

***

Jack waited beside Sienna's car as she lifted a red backpack into the trunk. He hated the thought of her leaving and wondered where she was going on her trip—she was travelling light—but he didn't want to pry. He'd done a lot of thinking over the past few days and he'd decided he was going to back off, but one look at her in that fairy dress and he was smitten again. He had fallen for her, and he didn't know what to do about it. All he knew was that he didn't want her to leave. She seemed a lot happier today, and it had been great to hear her laugh ring out. But he was going to tell her how he felt before the day was over.

Once her bag was stowed, he handed her the cake box and she opened the door and placed it carefully on the backseat. "I'll follow you," he said. "I don't quite remember where Blake and Ana live."

"Okay." She slipped into her car and Jack walked across to his bike. He pulled his boots on, swung his tights-clad leg over the seat, and waited for Sienna to start her car. After a couple of minutes, she opened the door and stood by the car.

"One, two, three," she muttered under her breath as he got closer.

"You haven't had your car fixed yet, have you?" he asked.

"No, I didn't have time." She frowned. "Bugger, I didn't need this today of all days." "Four…five…" She finished counting to ten. "It must have something to do with the battery, because if I get out and wait it always starts when I get back in."

Jack shrugged and waited for her to get back in. "That's not very logical. Make sure you have it serviced as soon as you get back from your holiday."

Sienna tried the engine again, but the only sound was a loud *click*. He waited while she tried again. As she climbed from the car, she shot him a regretful smile.

"I guess I'm going to miss the party after all."

Jack looked at her. Her brightly painted pink lips were clamped together tightly and her forehead was still wrinkled in a frown.

"Have you got a couple of smaller containers?" He grinned as the solution hit him.

"What for?"

"The cakes. If you've got some smaller containers they'll fit." He pointed to the panniers on each side of the bike.

"That's thoughtful of you," she said. "At least Faith won't miss out on the cakes. Show them to Thelma and Mitzi before they get eaten. And make sure they know I made them. Oh, I forgot, do you know them?"

Jack grinned at her. "No, I don't. But you can tell them yourself."

"I can?"

"Open your trunk." With a curious look, she did as he asked. He walked over and lifted out her backpack. "You've only got the cakes and that bag?"

"You think I'm going to go there on your motorbike?"

"Yes. You can wear the backpack and we'll put the cakes in there." He hoped like hell that she'd agree. "And then you won't miss out on the party. I'm sure someone will give you a lift to the airport later. And if not, I can take you on the bike."

His breath caught in his throat as her face broke into a wide grin.

"Serves me right for laughing at the thought of you riding up the highway in your costume. I guess you'd call it poetic justice. But I'll do it for Faith. I won't miss her birthday." She shook her head. "You know what? We'll both look ridiculous. But maybe that's just what I need."

Her laugh tinkled around him and he watched in appreciation as she grabbed the cake container from the car and hurried up the stairs. She wore pink tights beneath the short skirt, and her feet were encased in dainty silver slippers.

"You'll have to change your shoes," he called after her, trying to ignore the anticipation that was curling in his gut. Things were going his way.

A couple of minutes later, Sienna pulled the front door shut and ran lightly down the stairs. He waited at the bottom and took the two containers she passed him.

He looked down approvingly at her feet. She'd shed her sparkly slippers, and the pink tights were tucked into a pair of purple Doc Martens boots.

"Nice," he said. He couldn't take his eyes from her as she stared at him with a smile.

God, she is so beautiful.

"Take me to the party, Prince Charming."

###

Trying to keep his attention on the winding mountain curves was one of the hardest things Jack had ever done. Sienna's soft breasts pressed into his back and her hands clung to his waist. Every time a car tooted at them, she leaned forward and laughed in his ear, pressing even closer. It got to the point that he prayed no one else honked at them and she'd move back, because he'd be in no state to get off the bike wearing his pink Prince Charming tights. He knew now why they were called tights.

Sienna leaned forward and called out. "Two more driveways and then turn left into the third one. It's the driveway with the yellow mailbox."

Thank God, we're almost there.

Jack focused on the road, the bike, the sky, the trees, and the occasional glimpse of the silvery ocean at the bottom of the mountain—anything to forget the soft swells pressed up against his back. Up until he'd met Sienna, he'd been happy to be a loner. Life by himself had satisfied him. In fact, he'd needed the space. The thought of her leaving wrenched at his heart. If it meant keeping her by his side, he'd give up the gallery, his commissions, and if it was what she wanted of him, hell, he'd even go back into business and take life more seriously. Since he'd been out on the Sunny Coast, and since he'd fallen, yes, fallen in love with Sienna, he was prepared to change his ways.

Now was he able to convince her that he could?

Chapter Twenty-One

Jack steered the bike slowly to the end of a row of cars parked on the grass in front of Blake and Ana's cottage. The trip up from the coast had been exhilarating, and despite knowing what was waiting for her at the destination, Sienna had enjoyed every mile.

Sitting behind Jack, with her arms around his muscular frame, she'd wished the trip could go forever. But reality intruded as he drove the bike slowly through the gate. A tall, thin man with a craggy face and black hair stood leaning against the fence. He dropped his cigarette and buried it in the soft ground with the toe of his boot. Jack cut the motor and Sienna slid off the back of the bike. She stood beside him as he reached down and unclipped the helmet before lifting it from her head. She dropped her gaze from his and turned away without speaking. Her life was about to change, and she wasn't sure how she was going to handle this meeting. Conscious that Jack was watching curiously, she gave him a hesitant smile before walking over to the man who was waiting for her.

Uncle Renzo. My father.

He stepped toward her and held out his arms. Sienna caught a glimpse of Georgie standing on the porch watching, before the tears blurred her vision.

"*Mia figlia.*" My daughter. His voice was ragged, and she forgot all about Jack as her father held her close.

"I'm so sorry." His words hitched as she leaned into him and inhaled the familiar fragrance of this man who'd raised her. Tobacco and Old Spice aftershave mixed together in a familiar fragrance that brought back memories of sitting on his knee when he'd read her stories.

My father.

"I made a promise to Marjorie when she gave you to us, and Lucia made me keep it. So many times, I wished to tell you, but we could see how attached you and Georgie were. I knew if I broke it, Marjorie would come back and take Georgie."

"It's all right." Sienna stepped back and looked at her father. "I'm all right. I understand."

"And so do I." Sienna moved her gaze from Renzo to Georgie, who was standing beside Aunt Lucia on the porch, and happiness washed through her. Dressed in a similar outfit to Sienna, the pink of the fairy costume clashed ferociously with her tumbling red curls. Renzo held Sienna's hand tightly as they crossed the small patch of lawn and waited at the bottom of the steps. Aunt Lucia smiled down at them and Sienna could see the sheen of tears in her eyes. Georgie hurried down and jumped off the last step and stood beside her. Despite the tears in her eyes, she grinned and reached out to hug Sienna.

"Hey, sis."

Sienna hugged her back. "Hey to you too, sis."

"Let's go find the birthday girl," Sienna said, turning and looking around. "Ooh, I forgot about Jack."

Georgie squeezed her fingers. "He went around the back way. Love his costume. So what gives there?"

"I'll tell you later. You go find Ana and Faith, and I'll catch you up."

Jack was standing next to Blake at the edge of the lawn.

"Jack, did you remember the cakes?"

"No, I didn't. Sorry. I put your bag on the front porch, but I forgot the cakes."

"They might be a bit icky by now." Sienna followed Jack around to the front where the bike was parked. "You and Blake make a fine pair. Did you synchronise your costumes?"

A ripple ran through her at his sexy chuckle.

"No, coincidental." He looked down at his legs with a grimace. "He was the lucky one. He didn't have to wear tights. If I'd known he was dressing as Shrek, I could have come as Donkey."

"Or Princess Fiona." Sienna couldn't resist teasing him. "Seriously, Jack. You look gorgeous…and you know it."

She looked at him, letting her gaze sweep up from his boots. His long, muscular legs looked even bigger in the hot-pink tights, and when her gaze reached the tops of his thighs, she lifted it quickly to his face. He ran his hand through his hair, a gesture she was beginning to recognise when he was unsure of how to read her. She glanced around; no one was following them, and she put her hand on his arm. She couldn't help herself; she had to touch him.

"Thanks for the ride up. I enjoyed it very much."

"So did I." His gaze locked with hers and they shared a long look before Sienna dropped her eyes.

She cleared her throat and reached to the clip on the side of the pannier. "It was important that I come today. There was some family stuff I had to deal with. So, thank you."

He put his hand on top of hers as she undid the clip, and a warm tingle ran up her arm.

"No need to thank me. It's good to see a smile back on your face and…"

Sienna waited for him to continue, but he hesitated. He dropped his hand and waited while she unclipped the cover on the top of the compartment and reached in for the container.

"Great driving. All intact."

"Sienna?" The emotion in his voice sent panic spiralling through her, and she lifted her gaze. His green eyes captured hers and her breath caught.

No. She didn't want to hear it. She could read his mind before he even spoke.

God, she was acting like a teenager. She'd never let a man affect her like that before, and she wasn't about to start now. Men had been put in their right place from the minute she'd discovered them in her teens. She swallowed and straightened her shoulders.

"What?"

Jack took the cake container from her. "Once we go around the back and join in the party, you're going to get lost in the crowd. I want to tell you how I feel before the day ends, and right now is as good as ever." He reached out and took her shoulders with gentle fingers and Sienna's breath caught.

No.

"I've fallen for you, Sienna." Jack held her gaze, and the panic swelled in her chest. "I love being with you. I love watching you move. You're beautiful, you're talented. Forget the gallery, forget our work relationship…just trust how we feel."

Her throat closed as he slid his hands down her arms and held her elbows, pulling her closer.

"You do know what I am saying, don't you?"

She clung to him and his muscles flexed beneath the green Lycra of his shirt. She'd never seen him in anything but jeans and T-shirts, and she didn't want to think about how devastating he would look in a suit.

"I'm sorry." Her voice broke as she shook her head, and she saw the instant his face closed to her. "Jack, we might look like we believe in fairy tales, but there's no such thing as happy ever after."

No matter what he believed or how he thought he felt, Sienna wasn't going to be a part of it. She couldn't trust—even though her heart was screaming at her to listen to him. Marjorie had ensured enough hurt to last them all a lifetime, and Sienna didn't intend to add to it by listening to Jack. She pulled away from his grip and fought the tears that were threatening to fall.

"I'm sorry. I just can't. It's got nothing to do with you." She could give him that much. "It's not the gallery, it's not you, it's me."

She left him standing there. A beautiful man in a Prince Charming suit. A man she knew she loved but couldn't risk listening to.

###

As far as parties went, it turned into a huge celebration. Faith clapped her little hands with delight as her mother, Georgie, and Sienna formed a fairy ring around her and sang "Happy Birthday."

"Goodness, you look more like your daddy every day." Sienna swung her high and kissed the little girl's cheek as they finished singing.

"She sure does." Ana looked on proudly. "How are you, Sienna? Georgie came to me as soon as Marjorie left her." Ana's voice was quiet as she looped one arm around Sienna's shoulder. "I didn't call since it wasn't something that we could talk about on the phone, and I knew it was something you and Georgie needed to talk about together."

They moved toward the table where brightly-coloured presents were piled high. Faith's little friends ran around the table looking at the presents, squealing with excitement.

"I'm fine. Really, I am. The last few days have answered a lot of questions about my life and where I'm heading." Sienna glanced up and heat ran through her as she caught Jack's intent gaze fixed on her. He was standing on the other side of Blake. She elbowed Ana and giggled. "Look at them…whoever would have thought that? Remember the first day the pair of them came into the shop and the wheelbarrows fell on you?"

Ana smiled. "I do. So, what's happened between you and Jack?"

"You and Georgie are nosy. Remember, I'm the private one who doesn't share." She softened her words as she tapped Ana with her fairy wand. "There's nothing between us. I'll tell all when I get back."

But what was there to tell? she wondered. The feelings she had for Jack had overwhelmed her. They were unfamiliar to her and she wasn't sure she could handle rejecting him. Every time she caught his eye, her heart felt as though it was going to burst out of her chest, and her legs trembled.

They stood together as friends came over to give Faith a birthday kiss. Aldo and Maria, Joe and Magda, and many of the people she'd known all her life. She knew Jack was watching her. She couldn't stop looking over there—his gaze was fixed on her, and a tremble ran down her back. Renzo stood beside her and kept his arm around her shoulders, and a small measure of happiness filled the empty place in her chest. Knowing the truth had settled her and seemed to have taken away the distance she had always sensed that Renzo kept between them.

What Marjorie had done was a good thing. A sharp pang of sadness shot through her; it might have been good if she'd been here and there was forgiveness all around, but Georgie hadn't heard from her mother again after she'd told her the truth and disappeared with Sienna's cash. They just had to accept that Marjorie had her own problems and they couldn't do anything about it. She'd have to watch Georgie and make sure she was okay with it.

Mitzi and Thelma came over to say hello, and she was enveloped in a cloud of lavender perfume and happy laughter. They were surrounded by children. Blake's nephews and niece had come to the party and were dressed as fairy-tale characters.

"Is there cakes?" Billy, the second youngest of the five tugged at her leg. "Ana said you had the cakes."

"Yes Billy, there are lots of cakes. Did you see them?" Sienna turned to the elderly sisters and kissed each of their soft, papery cheeks. "They're over near the table with the presents."

Billy ran off and Mitzi grabbed Sienna's arm. "Yes, and we saw your Prince Charming, too. Are you going to introduce us to your man?"

"My man?" Her stomach dropped. She had to nip this in the bud before Thelma and Mitzi got their hands on Jack and gave him the third degree and told him every detail of her life.

Mitzi pointed to Jack. "Prince Charming."

"Not *my* man. Jack's simply a friend who gave me a ride up here when my car wouldn't start." The two elderly women exchanged a glance, and she knew they didn't believe a word she was saying.

She escaped before they could ask more.

She was broke, thanks to Marjorie, and she'd quit her job. All she had was her house and a few boxes of frogs. And she'd offered her house to Jack…if he accepted her offer, she wouldn't have that either.

But before she left, Sienna wanted to share the news with the whole family…and their close friends. A lot of the guests had left and there was mainly family left. Sienna looked around for Jack. She wanted him to be close by. She walked over to Renzo and stood on her toes and whispered in her father's ear. "Ready?"

Renzo nodded before he called for quiet. Their family and close friends gathered around. Lucia stood beside them and held his hand. A small group of interested faces looked at her and for a moment, her vision blurred as tears filled her eyes. But they were happy tears.

"This week I found my father." Sienna's breath hitched as she caught Jack's eye. A frown wrinkled his brow.

Sienna turned to Georgie with a smile. "And Georgie and I finally discovered this week why we are so different. It's a complicated story, but I'll tell you all about that later. Today is for Faith's birthday." She turned to Renzo. "All I need to say is I have found my father and even though Georgie and I have found out we're not blood sisters...to each other we always will be true sisters."

As the party wound up, Sienna looked around for Jack, but he was nowhere to be seen. A hollow feeling settled in her stomach when she wondered if he'd left without saying good-bye. Maybe all this family stuff had been too much for him? Maybe it wasn't his scene? It had been something she needed to be a part of, and she was sorry if it had bothered him. Maybe it was too much for his laidback attitude. When she thought about it, he hadn't told her much about his family, but she'd sensed there was a problem there.

"Are you going to get changed before you leave for the airport?" Blake reached for Faith, and Sienna glanced at her watch.

"We'd better get a move on."

"Before you do, Jack was wondering if you'd see him before he leaves. He's out by his bike." Blake hoisted Faith up onto his shoulders. "Come on, young lady, let's go check out your new toys."

Georgie and Ana followed him inside and Sienna slowly made her way over to where Jack had parked. He'd changed out of his costume and into a pair of jeans and a snug black T-shirt. Standing beside the bike, he looked as sexy as hell. Deep down, Sienna was afraid. Her emotions had been on a rollercoaster for the past week, and she had to dig deep for strength. She couldn't hook up with Jack for a lot of reasons, no matter how much she wanted to.

"I thought you'd left."

"Blake invited me to stay, but I've got some business I have to attend to. I've postponed the golf game. I wanted to wish you a good trip…and say no hard feelings. I guess I read too much into things."

He took a step closer to her and a shiver ran down her back. "I'll look after the gallery while you're gone."

She shook her head. "It's your gallery, Jack."

He ignored her. She backed away as his intent became clear, but she wasn't quick enough. His warm fingers glided up to her face and cupped her gently as his mouth settled on hers. Sienna stretched up onto her toes and kissed him right back.

It was a sweet kiss. A kiss made for lovers, and she couldn't resist his mouth, losing herself in the sweetness that she didn't want to succumb to. Warmth flooded through her.

By the time Jack lifted his head, Sienna had managed to get a grip on her emotions. She dropped her hands; she hadn't even been conscious of holding on to him as his lips had explored hers.

"It would have been so much easier if you hadn't done that," she said.

He stared at her for several heartbeats before his soft reply. "Probably, but I wanted to say good-bye…properly."

He swung his leg over the bike, turned the key, and the engine fired with a throaty roar.

Before he could put his helmet on, Sienna grabbed his arm.

"Jack?"

Those beautiful green eyes held hers and she swallowed.

"Good-bye." It broke her heart, but Sienna tried to put conviction into her words. She wanted him to know she was really saying good-bye.

"For now." Jack stared at her for a moment longer before he lifted his helmet on.

Sienna stood for a long time until the bike and its rider were a small black speck in the distance. For the first time in her life, her heart yearned for another. A little niggle of regret snaked its way through her thoughts.

For now?

Chapter Twenty-Two

The flight from Maroochydore to Tamworth was delayed, and Ana and Georgie made the most of the time, hitting Sienna with a barrage of questions. Finally, they realised they weren't going to get the answers they wanted from her. Sienna stared off into space as Ana and Georgie chattered away beside her. Change was in the wind, just like it had been when they'd sold their business to Blake, and Ana and Blake got together. Ana had just told them that she and Blake were moving to Melbourne for a while to help out Jack's father while he wound down his business interests.

"But it's only temporary? Right?" Sienna hated the thought of them moving so far away.

"Yes, it is…and just think of the galleries you can visit when you come to see us." Ana squeezed her arm. "You will visit, won't you?"

"Of course I will." Sienna laughed. "I need to find a job first." A little voice niggled at her.

You could always stay at the gallery and work for Jack.

"What about you, Georgie? What are you going to do?" Sienna asked.

A new manager was coming in to oversee the Maleny store while Blake was away, and she wondered whether Georgie would stay.

"I've booked an around-the-world air ticket. As soon as the new guy is settled in, I'm off. I may see Machu Picchu for my next birthday yet." Georgie squeezed her hand. "It's about time I learned to stand on my own two feet."

Despite all the change and her own uncertainty of what the future held for her after she finished up at Jack's gallery, Sienna felt settled—almost. If only she could keep Jack's face out of her thoughts. She put her hand up to her lips. After he kissed her this afternoon, he'd smiled at her, and her toes curled now as she remembered the feelings that had run through her.

Georgie tipped her head to the side. "Now what about you? Maybe the sale fell through and you say you're going to leave, but I know when there's something going on."

"I'll tell you about it when I come home next week."

Georgie narrowed her eyes. "You're still having your exhibition before you leave, aren't you?"

Sienna shook her head. "No, I cancelled it. I gave some money to Marjorie, and now I can't afford it. I wasn't ready for it anyway. Too much of a rush to get it finished." She didn't like the thoughtful look that Georgie shot her as she picked up her bag.

"Don't you go meddling in anything that doesn't concern you, okay?" She hugged her cousin first, and then Ana. "Thelma and Mitzi are bad enough. Just let me sort my own life out. Remember, I'm more than happy being alone." She looked at Georgie. "I am."

***

Jack leaned back against the front door of the gallery, his legs stretched out in front of him. The cold marble tiles pressed against the backs of his legs and he shivered. All the way back from the party on Sunday night, Sienna's good-bye had echoed through his head. He'd known she meant more than a casual good-bye and was trying to tell him something more.

He'd come straight back to the gallery, planning to stay there until he found something more permanent. He'd spent the first night castigating himself for telling Sienna how he felt too soon. He should have given her more time, but he'd been scared of letting her go without telling her how he felt. And he'd blown it.

No matter how it turned out, he'd been honest. Her words of a couple of weeks ago stuck in his mind.

"Your family is loaded, and you have a playboy reputation."

She said she'd had no idea why he saw her as a challenge, because he knew now the challenge was getting her to love him back. But would his honesty give them both happiness? After a sleepless night, he unlocked the storage area and pulled his biggest sculpture into the studio. He managed to lose himself as the creative muse kicked in and thoughts of Sienna fled—almost. It was as though she was there with him as he shaped and moulded the metal. He'd smiled to himself as he made his perfect 'pancake' mix of enamel.

He pushed himself to his feet and pulled out his phone and snapped a series of pictures of his creature from all angles. A creature it was—certainly different from any of Sienna's small creatures. His had the shape of a phoenix rising from the ashes, but from the front view it appeared to be a dragon, the small pieces of scarlet enamel looking like fire surrounding its long jaw.

He messaged his parents and attached one of the photographs. A short message that he knew would please his father.

Beat the deadline by three days, Dad.

His phone beeped almost immediately, and a surge of satisfaction rushed through him.

Proud of you, son.

He stared down at the phone. No. He was going to give her space while she was away. As he held the phone, it rang and he looked down at the unfamiliar number for a moment before taking the call.

"Jack?"

"Yes?"

"It's Georgie. I was hoping you were around." Disappointment hit him; for a moment he thought maybe Sienna had gotten hold of him. He wasn't going to push her. He'd decided what he wanted; she had to come to him of her own accord.

Jack ran a hand across his face. Since he'd been immersed in the enamelling, he hadn't showered or changed. His stomach grumbled and he realised he hadn't eaten since yesterday.

"I'm coming to town and I was hoping I could meet with you?"

"Sure, what time will you be in town?"

They made arrangements to meet at the coffee shop where he'd eaten with Sienna on his first day in town. He was about to end the call when Georgie continued.

"And Jack? I hope you don't mind me stepping in. I hope I was reading you right when I saw the way you looked at my sister?"

###

Jack ordered the biggest plate of pancakes and bacon from the menu and was on his third coffee by the time Georgie arrived. She slid into the chair opposite him and smiled.

"You look like you haven't slept."

"I've been working."

"Missing Sienna?"

"You are spot-on there." Jack frowned as he forked the last piece of bacon from his plate. "The place isn't the same without her."

"Sienna will kill me when she finds out what I'm going to tell you." Georgie settled back into her chair and looked at him as the waitress poured her a coffee. "But I want her to be happy. She's kidding herself that she can ignore the way she feels about you."

Jack's fork clattered to the table as he stared back at her. "Are you sure?"

"Yes, I know my sister. You have to know a bit about our background to understand why she protects herself so much."

Jack's world filled with colour. For the first time he noticed the bright flowers spilling from the half wine casks scattered around the terrace they were sitting on. Even though he'd been working with colours for the past two days, everything apart from his sculpture had looked grey and bleak.

"I know she cares about you—otherwise I wouldn't be here." Georgie stared at him and her words filled him with happiness. "Sienna's always been the tough one and so independent, but I've seen the way she looks at you."

For the next half hour, Georgie told him of their family and how she was sure that the only reason Sienna was pushing Jack away was to protect herself from being hurt. Knowing that it was Sienna's personal circumstances that had caused her so much angst relieved the burden that pressed on Jack. He carried a lot of guilt because he'd changed his mind about selling the gallery, and then Arielle's arrival had topped it all off.

"Once she's been to Tamworth and accepted what she finds there, she'll be ready to listen to you. I promise. I know her almost as well as I know myself." Georgie had filled in a lot of the gaps for him about why Sienna kept herself so private. "She doesn't share her emotions easily, but I know how she feels about you. Trust me."

Even though Sienna had said good-bye, the way she had kissed him before he left the party had filled him with a smidgeon of hope. Knowing that his actions had nothing to do with why Sienna had cancelled her show was a relief. A glimmer of an idea began to form as he thought of a way to make her happy.

"Georgie, have you got a day or two to spare before Sienna comes home?"

###

It had taken a long time to get things organised. Jack knew what he wanted to do, and the conversation with Georgie had nailed it.

Now all he had to do was persuade Sienna to trust him. When he heard about the payoff she'd made to Georgie's mother, the final piece had fallen into place. Even if Sienna couldn't buy the gallery, he'd give her a half-share on the condition that she'd manage it for him. Hell, he'd even share the studio with her. And he'd share his life with her.

If she'd have him.

Maybe he was kidding himself, but he really hoped that the welcome he and Georgie had planned would convince Sienna where his heart lay. His future—their future—depended on the next couple of hours. Now all he was waiting for was the text from Georgie to say they were on their way.

Jack flicked the collar of his white shirt and straightened his tie as he looked around the gallery with satisfaction.

THE TROUBLE WITH JACK

Chapter Twenty-Three

The week in Tamworth reaffirmed Sienna's belief in herself as an artist. She'd wandered around art galleries, taken in a few exhibitions, and learned to relax. She'd stayed in bed late and eaten in a different restaurant every night. But she hadn't slept. Despite being there to find closure about her family and say good-bye to her mother, her mind had been filled with thoughts of Jack, wondering what he was doing and how he was coping with the gallery.

By Wednesday, when she'd picked up the phone for the tenth time to call, she finally admitted to herself that if he'd have her back, she'd keep working for him. She could accept his casual interest in the gallery. And he had a work ethic, no matter how much he pretended he was laidback and didn't care. The argument went back and forth in her head until she sighed and cleared her thoughts. If she didn't get some sleep, she'd be no good working for anyone.

And he'd said he loved her. That had to count for something.

She was filled with uncertainty, and it didn't sit well with her. Sienna, who always knew what she wanted and went for it; Sienna, who had been secure and comfortable where she was in life was struggling with the knowledge that she'd finally fallen for someone and fallen hard.

The half hour she had spent in the small cemetery beside the plaque with her mother's name on it finally brought her closure. This woman was someone she'd never known. She had no regrets and bore no malice. She'd done her research; there was no other family to look up. Her grandparents were dead, and her mother had been an only child. There was nothing for her in Tamworth apart from a lonely grave.

Back on the Sunshine Coast was a man who had kissed her and told her to think about that kiss. A man who loved her. She had thought about him constantly, and a feeling of lightness filled her as she came to a decision. Her true family was back at Maleny. Her heart—she finally admitted to herself—was with a green-eyed Prince Charming in Noosa.

Sienna's flight arrived late Friday night, too late to text Georgie to pick her up, so she stayed in a hotel and called the next morning.

"Can you pick me up and take me to Maleny?" Sienna stared out over the bay from her hotel window. It was good to be back on the coast.

"I'll do better than that. I'll drive you all the way to Noosa. I'll be there in an hour." Georgie disconnected before Sienna could say she'd planned on spending the weekend catching up with Blake and Ana before they moved to Melbourne. It had nothing to do with her nervousness about seeing Jack again.

She checked out and headed down to the restaurant to have a coffee while she waited.

"Blake and Ana are away for the weekend," Georgie said as she drove past the exit to Maleny..

"I'll spend some time with Renzo and Lucia instead."

"They're away, too."

"Who's running the restaurant?" Sienna had never known Renzo to take a day off when they were growing up.

"One of the chefs, apparently." Georgie shrugged.

"Take the next exit. I'll go and see Thelma and Mitzi."

"They're away, too."

Sienna narrowed her eyes. "They never go away."

"They are. They got invited to a…party."

Sienna was curious, but Georgie didn't say any more for a while, focusing on the road ahead.

"So, you had a good trip?" Georgie shot her a glance.

"Yes, went to lots of galleries and had a good break."

"You look relaxed. What are your plans now?"

"I'm still not sure." Sienna didn't want to share just yet in case things didn't work out.

Georgie took the exit into Coolum from the motorway and Sienna looked across at her.

"Time for a coffee before I take you to the lake," Georgie said with a grin.

"It's only five minutes to my house." Now that she was almost home, Sienna was keen to get there. "I'll make you a coffee there. Or better still we can go into Noosa and I can…"

"Can what?"

"Nothing." She'd been going to say call in at the gallery. "I'm not sure if my car will start. That's why Jack gave me a ride to the party. She's been a bit temperamental."

"A bit like her owner." Georgie shot her a grin.

"Thanks, sis." Sienna waited as Georgie found a parking spot. "I guess we're having coffee here."

They found a coffee shop in the surf club and Sienna examined the art on the walls while they waited for their order and Georgie sent some texts. She was up to something. Sienna knew her all too well.

"Not a new man?" She gestured to the phone.

"What? Ah, no. Just some texts for the…er…store."

"Just be careful, Georgie. No more Cals, promise?"

"No more *Coles*, that's for sure." Georgie laughed. "Hurry up, finish your coffee and I'll drop you at home."

"We just got here." Sienna narrowed her eyes. "Please tell me you haven't done something I'm going to hate."

"*I've* done nothing. And that's all I have to say on the matter. Now come on." Georgie picked up her phone and purse and waited for Sienna to finish her coffee.

Sienna knew Georgie was up to something. She folded her arms and didn't say a word as Georgie went past her turn off and drove into Noosa and turned into Hastings Street.

She parked the car and turned to Sienna. "Have you got your lipstick handy? And fluff up your hair. Someone's got a little surprise for you."

"Who?"

"You'll see. Now stop asking questions, make yourself pretty, and follow me."

Bemused, and slightly nervous because she knew Jack was involved, she let Georgie lead her along the street until they turned back onto the main street and headed toward Sea

View Gallery. The tourists were out in force this morning and a large crowd was gathered outside the gallery looking at the window display. Sienna thought back, trying to remember what she'd put on display before she'd left last week.

A group of white bowls certainly did nothing to get that much attention.

"I like the red one with the dangly leg." The woman's voice carried across as they finally cleared the crowd and stood at the door. Sienna looked up and her ears began to buzz. She put her hand up to her chest.

"Oh my God."

"Don't you go fainting on me, Sienna."

Her heart almost stopped as she saw the man who was waiting beside the door. Jack was dressed in a dark suit and white shirt.

Oh God, he is so gorgeous.

The look in his eyes banished the last uncertainty that lingered in Sienna's mind. He reached out for her and ran the pad of his thumb over her bottom lip just as he had a few days ago.

"Close your mouth and stop gaping, Sienna, so I can kiss you hello."

She stepped toward him and moved her hand up to his smooth-shaven cheek.

"I missed you." Jack's deep green eyes were fixed on hers, and the noise of the street and the chattering tourists faded into the background as he filled her vision.

"Before you kiss me hello, I want to tell you what I found." She kept her voice low and Jack lowered his head closer to hers to listen to her words. "I fought this so much. Not because of you, but because of where I came from. I knew I was falling in love with you and it terrified me. I couldn't trust those feelings that I could be happy and that it would last."

Jack's cheek was against hers and she closed her eyes as she revelled in the feel of his skin against hers.

"But you taught me how to feel happy again, and I know I can trust you. You made me laugh when things were tough even though I didn't share them with you." She turned her face, and his lips were almost touching hers.

His warm breath caressed her skin.

"I was going to wait no matter how long it took. I fell in love with you all over again when you glared at me the first night in Fish

Divine." Jack's voice sent a shiver down Sienna's back and she opened her eyes and tipped her head back to look at him.

"Again?"

"It was the same feeling I had when I saw you the first time a couple of years back. I just didn't know what it was then. We're meant to be together. Have I convinced you of that yet or do I have to lock you away in my Prince Charming castle to convince you?"

"Maybe you'd like to try a little harder to convince me right now?" It was as though they were in a fairy-tale world of their own making. She closed her eyes while Jack held her face gently and his lips finally slid onto hers. Warmth stole over her and spread through her. Only their lips and hands were touching, but a wealth of feeling poured through Sienna when the pressure of Jack's lips increased on hers. She sank into the pleasure until he murmured against her mouth. "We have to go inside."

"To the sofa bed in the studio?" She looked up at him and let a saucy grin spread across her face.

"Er...I don't think it's quite the right moment for that, but please hold that thought for later."

Her gaze stayed on him as he took her hand and tucked it in the corner of his arm.

"Follow me."

Jack led her inside as Georgie held the door open.

***

The banner stretched across the gallery spelled out **A VISIT WITH CREATURES, with SIENNA SACCHI** written in scrolling letters along the bottom. A table laden with finger food and champagne glasses was along the back of the gallery, and the shelves she could see through the mass of people were filled with her frogs and tiny creatures. Not as many as she'd planned for, but still enough to look good.

A small cheer went up as Sienna paused in the doorway. Jack's hand was against her back and she reached behind and held it tightly as she looked around. Renzo and Lucia, Thelma and Mitzi, Aldo and Maria, Joe and Magda, and Blake and Ana stood at the front of the large group of people filling the gallery.

"The guest of honour is here." Renzo stepped forward and kissed her cheek. "I'm very proud of my daughter. Her work is amazing."

Sienna shook her head, unable to believe what she was seeing. She turned to Jack and grinned again as she took in the uncharacteristic white shirt, and tie and suit trousers. Her heart was thudding, and the familiar tremble was back in her legs, and it didn't have as much to do with the shock of seeing her exhibition set up as much as this sexy man holding her as though he'd never let her go,

"Where's my Jack gone?" she whispered with a smile.

Joy spread across his face and another small cheer went up as Sienna lifted her arms up around his neck and pressed her lips to his in front of everyone who mattered to her.

"Your Jack's right here and he's not going anywhere," he murmured.

Sienna dropped her head and buried it in his neck for a moment until she regained her composure. When she turned, she caught Georgie giving Jack a thumbs-up gesture.

"So, I guess Georgie spilled the beans about why I cancelled the show?" She held his gaze and Jack nodded.

"She did, but that was only part of it. I wanted to have Sienna Sacchi, amazing artist, and her frogs, to be the first exhibition at *our* gallery."

"Our gallery?"

"Oh, there's lots more I have to tell you." Jack held her hand tightly as she looked around in amazement. Jack—she assumed he'd set up the show—had done a wonderful job of spacing her pieces, and the lighting was incredible. "Everything else can wait except for one thing."

"What's that? What else can you possibly have for me?" She gestured around the room. "Apart from all of this." She let out a small cry as she noticed the large sculpture just inside the foyer. "Oh, you finished. You met your deadline."

Jack shook his head with a cheeky grin that almost curled her toes. "I finished one. I can't get too organised. Just one more thing…I have to tell the artist how much I love her again before the guests take all her attention."

"I love you too." She stretched up to her toes and kissed him again. "While ever you're here, Prince Charming, no one else will get more of my attention than you."

Jack's eyes widened as he looked over her head, almost lost for words. "Oh my God."

"You make me so happy." Sienna smiled up at him. He was always happy and smiling; that was one of the things she loved about him. Now his eyes were alight with pleasure even as he looked over her head.

Yes, I love him. It was a wonderful feeling that coursed through her veins.

"Oh. My God," he said again.

"I love the way nothing ever fazes you," she said.

"Oh yes it does," he said. He stared over her shoulder and Sienna followed his gaze.

"Chris Hemsworth just walked through the door. *Our* gallery's hit the big time."

Epilogue

"Hurry up, Jack."

"I'm almost ready." His voice was muffled and Sienna grinned. It sounded like he was still in the bathroom towelling his hair.

She stood at the door of the Park Hyatt Hotel bathroom as she waited for Jack to come out. Three months of sharing the management of the gallery, as well as sharing her house, and her bedroom, with him had taught her some of his quirks.

He hated being late. As much as he denied that he was working and co-managing with her, and that he hated deadlines, Sienna had seen a different side to Jack over the past few months. Scheduling shows and liaising with artists, while she did the day-to-day running of the gallery, he had demonstrated the business skills he'd kept hidden and still wouldn't admit to having. He'd met his deadline and today they were in Melbourne for the unveiling of his sculptures in the entry of the building in Federation Square.

"Jack, your parents are waiting in the foyer. Are you almost ready?"

"I'm coming. Where's my shirt?"

"I don't know. It's your shirt." Sienna still preserved her prickly side, but Jack saw through it every time. She loved sharing her life with him and was looking forward to this special day with him.

Finally, he appeared in the doorway in casual chinos and a T-shirt.

"You can't go dressed like that." She frowned at him and he grinned his sexy grin that always melted her resistance. His hair was mussed, and he looked like he was going to the beach, and she said as much.

"It's my day and I'll wear what I'm comfortable in." He tapped her on the behind as they walked toward the door. "I didn't tell you what to wear to yours, did I?"

"That's because I didn't know I was having one." Sienna stopped and turned to Jack as he reached for the door. She slipped her arms around his waist as she looked up at him.

"Before we go and you get lost in the adoring masses, I want to tell you how much I love you. "She stood on her tiptoes and pressed her lips against his, revelling in the feel of this man she loved so much. "And to wish you an amazing day." She kissed him again. "That's for luck."

"If you keep that up, we are going to be late." Jack swooped her into his arms and sat down in the fancy antique chair by the door. "But keep going, I think I need more luck."

Sienna giggled as Jack settled her comfortably in his lap and trailed his lips down the side of her neck.

"You are incorrigible. I didn't think you wanted to be late," she said.

"I'm the guest of honour. A few minutes won't hurt."

His lips reached hers and Sienna closed her eyes. She'd laughed so much over the past three months. Being with Jack filled her with a joy she'd never experienced before, and he amazed her every day with the ways he could make her laugh. His hands lingered on her skin, and she swallowed a smile as the phone rang on the antique table beside the chair they were perched in. She slipped off his lap and stood in front of him. "Come on, your parents are waiting."

Jack rose reluctantly and looped his arm around her shoulders as they walked down to the corridor to the elevator.

"Do you think Chris might come?"

THE END

If you enjoyed Jack and Sienna's story stay posted for Ana and Blake, and Georgie and Liam's stories later in 2020. Subscribe to Annie's newsletter on her website: http://www.annieseaton.net

Also by Annie Seaton

Whitsunday Dawn
Undara

Porter Sisters Series

Kakadu Sunset
Daintree
Diamond Sky
Hidden Valley (2021)

Pentecost Island Series (2020)

Pippa

Eliza

Nell

Tamsin

Evie

Cherry… and more to come

Bondi Beach Love Series

Beach House

Beach Music

Beach Walk

Beach Dreams

Prickle Creek Series

Her Outback Cowboy

Her Outback Surprise

His Outback Nanny

His Outback Temptation

Second Chance Bay Series

Her Outback Playboy

Her Outback Protector

Her Outback Haven **(FINALIST for the NZ KORU AWARD 2020)**

Her Outback Paradise

Love Across Time Series

Come Back to Me

Follow Me

Lucy's Story (2020)

Others

The Trouble with Paradise

The Trouble with Jack

Deadly Secrets

Adventures in Time

Silver Valley Witch

The Emerald Necklace

Ten Days in Tuscany

Worth the Wait

Full Circle

ANNIE SEATON

About the Author

Author of the Year Ausrom Readers' Choice 2014

Best Established Author Ausrom Readers' Choice 2015

Finalist for Author of the Year, Book of the Year, Cover of the Year, Ausrom Readers' Choice 2016

Best Established Author, Ausrom Readers' Choice 2017

Book of the Year (Whitsunday Dawn) Ausrom Readers' Choice Awards 2018

Annie lives in Australia, on the beautiful north coast of New South Wales. She sits in her writing chair and looks out over the tranquil Pacific Ocean. She has fulfilled her lifelong dream of becoming an author and is producing books at a prolific rate.

She writes contemporary romance and loves telling the stories that always have a happily ever after. She lives with her very own hero of many years and they share their home with Toby, the naughtiest dog in the universe, and Barney, the rag doll kitten, who hides when the grandchildren come to visit.

Stay up to date with her latest releases at her website: http://www.annieseaton.net

If you would like to stay up to date with Annie's releases, subscribe to her newsletter on her website.

THE TROUBLE WITH JACK

Lightning Source UK Ltd.
Milton Keynes UK
UKHW010633070820
367857UK00001B/54